Tales of

Beyond Our World

Collected Short Stories of

Laura Vosika

with Chris Powell

Cover Design: Laura Vosika
Cover Photography: Chris R. Powell

Contact editors@gabrielshornpress.com

Published in Minneapolis, Minnesota by Gabriel's Horn Press

First printing:
2021 Printed in
the United
States.
For sales, please visit www.gabrielshornpress.com

ISBN: 978-1-938990-73-1

Other Books by Laura Vosika

The Blue Bells Chronicles: a tale of time travel....
- *Blue Bells of Scotland*
- *The Minstrel Boy*
- *The Water is Wide*
- *Westering Home*
- *The Battle is O'er*

Food and Feast in the World of the Blue Bells Chronicles: a gastronomic historic poetic musical romp in thyme

Glenmirril Garden: original music in the style of Celtic jigs and reels (with Judd Knauss)

Go Home and Practice: a record book for music students and musicians for better progress

On Wings of Light and Love: poetry and essays on love (with Chris R. Powell)

Gabriel's Horn Poetry Anthologies, collator/editor
- *Startled by JOY: 2019*
- *Startled by NATURE: 2020*
- *Startled by LOVE: 2021*

Tales of Things Beyond Our World

Introduction

Stories of the mysterious are as old as storytelling—as old as humanity. From time immemorial, tales have been told of ghosts, vampires, werewolves, time slips, fairies, redcaps, trolls, mysterious villages that exist outside of time, doppelgangers, people with strange powers and knowledge, events that seem to recur as if imprinted on the air itself—and much more that is beyond the ability of science to explain.

Hundreds of years ago, there was the story of King Herla. In it, King Herla agrees that if the Troll King attends his wedding, he will attend the Troll King's wedding in return. After feasting with the Troll King in his underworld realm for three days, King Herla and his men rise back to the upper world —only to find that 300 years have passed. This same story is told in many variations around the world.

And let's take a deep dive into vampires! Cultures around the world and throughout history tell stories of vampire-like creatures. Dracula was not the first—nor was the concept thought up by Bram Stoker. While the world now thinks of Transylvania as the home of vampires, in truth, Ireland has its *Abhartach*—an evil dwarf who continued to rise from his grave after being 'killed.' It has the *Dearg Due*, a neglected wife of a cruel chieftain who rose from her grave to seek revenge.

In Scotland, William of Newburgh recounts the story in his *Historia rerum Anglicarum,* his famous historical chronicles, of the 'Hundpriest' or dog priest of Melrose Abbey who rose from his grave at night. It is worth stressing that William of Newburgh, a monk, was not writing folklore. He is, even today, regarded by modern historians as an authoritative and accurate source on his time. He prided himself on accuracy in reporting. No fake news for him!

There are similar stories in Spain, Germany, England, Croatia, Romania, Slovenia, Slovakia, the Czech Republic, Bulgaria, Urkraine, across the Slavic countries, in Iceland, Hungary, Greece.

West Africa's *Ashanti* have their *asanbosam.* The Ewe people of Togo and Ghana speak of the *adze.* The Betsileo people of Madagascar have tales of the *ramanga*—a living vampire who drinks the blood of nobles (and eats their nail clippings....that one's a little different.)

Stories of vampire-like creatures abound throughout the Asian world, as well.

While stories of vampires were known throughout most of the medieval world, they go farther back than that. Tales of blood-drinking undead go back to ancient times, to ancient Greece, Mesopotamia, and India, and even to Hebrew tales.

If we dig into other topics today regarded as paranormal—of ghosts, of people waking in the wrong century, of mysterious doings—we will find they, too, have been with us for a very long time.

Another universal story is that of a great flood. Virtually every culture has a similar story. Sociologists suggest that the universality of this story suggests something really did happen. How could all these people, so far removed from each other, all make up the same story? I ask the same of our own stories of the strange, of things we don't understand: If such stories are told around the world and from time immemorial—of vampire-like creatures, of ghosts, of strange time lapses—*Why?*

Why do so many people tell this same story?

How did so many people think it up?

I doubt we can say definitively. But it's at least worth asking: did so many people 'think up' the same story because the stories are more real than even the most avid ghost-hunter and horror tale enthusiast would like to believe?

Then again—maybe our Creator knows we're curious people with a thirst for a good story and so just planted these same ideas around the world to play with us! Maybe aliens really did come to earth and as a cosmic joke on the infant human race planted these stories around the globe!

What I think most people can agree to is that Hamlet was right in saying, *There are more things in heaven and earth, Horatio, than are dreamt of in your philosophy.*

Or in the words of 2 Corinthians 4:18: *So we fix our eyes not on what is seen, but on what is unseen, since what is seen is temporary, but what is unseen is eternal.*

WHY WE'RE FASCINATED

Why has mankind remained fascinated with these things for all time? I think the reasons vary and any one person may have different reasons at the same time or at different times in their lives.

1. A desire for something outside our drab ordinary lives.

2. An attempt to make sense of the world around us. These stories tell us life is not always what we thought it was.

3. Intellectual curiosity. What really *is* in our world.

I believe we are drawn to question our universe and the world around us. I believe it's because deep inside, each of us knows the truth—there is more to this world than what we see around us.

And why are we drawn to the dark, the dangerous, the frightening? Is it because we all have our fears? It's a topic discussed by many psychologists.

I personally think that one reason is that we *know* the world can be a dark and dangerous place. In a good scary story of the unnatural, the unexpected, we put ourselves in the shoes of the protagonist and we think about how we might handle the dangerous and unexpected things that we know can happen in life.

MY OWN EXPERIENCES

In my own life, I've had only a very few such experiences. I think most people have had more. But they were certainly enough to make me ask what I really experienced. Were they real or flights of imagination? Some would argue one and some, the other.

Perhaps my earliest experience of knowing someone who believed she'd experienced a ghost came when I was 12. My mother, by a funny coincidence, gave birth to my youngest sister the same day as our neighbor down the street in Duluth, where we had just moved, and so learned this story. The woman's house had originally been the carriage house to the home next door. In the 1920s, it was said, the groom who worked there went crazy and started shooting out the windows. The police arrived and shot back. The stories differ on whether he was seriously injured, or killed.

What the homeowner could say for sure was that there was a red stain on the floor in the lower level where he was shot, that would not come out with any amount of scrubbing.

She could tell us that one day she was alone with her two very young children when she heard very distinct, clear steps coming up the wooden stairs that led to the kitchen where she was feeding her children. Her husband's dog, a hunting dog, rose, the hair on its neck and back standing on end, and looked down the stairs, growling.

It will come as no surprise to any reader of a book such as this that, when she looked down the stairs, the footsteps stopped and there was no one there. Disquieting—but perhaps a better outcome than finding a stranger there who shouldn't be?

The final incident (that I know of) was a day the woman was in the lower level doing her laundry and was suddenly overcome with the worst feeling of someone watching her. Being a person who wants to know the truth and knows that our minds and emotions and fears can do all sorts of things to us—I see 'the feeling of being watched' as no proof of anything. What I find interesting about the incident is that it was one in a string of experiences she had in this house. It was also the final. She ran upstairs and prayed for a long time over the house. She never again experienced anything there.

I can say that I have never been the sort to *want* ghostly or paranormal experiences. I've often told my music students I love music because it's *safe!* Therefore, I am glad that my personal experiences have been much milder than many we hear.

I once felt a bed cover yanked off my bed while I was spending the night at my friend's house in one of Duluth's older homes. Was it a ghost or did her dog drag it off, somehow unseen by me when I sat up in surprise to see what had caused it? I only know there was no one around.

In 2008, I first visited Scotland for a research trip. Because one scene in my book included Shawn going into the middle of a ring of standing stones, hoping for their reputed mystical powers to bring him home, I went to standing stones and went into the center. There, I felt a distinct force pushing on my chest. I can't say it was overt. It was subtle. But it was without a doubt there.

I don't believe I stepped into those stones expecting anything. I'd never believed standing stones had any inherent mystical power. So I didn't merely experience something I expected or hoped for and thus conjure it up. Then again—our minds are powerful things (not to mention very playful with us sometimes!)

On my second research trip to Scotland, a friend and I stayed at the hostel near the ruins of Lochranza on the Isle of Aran. Inside those ruins, the stairs going to the second level are barred off. I took numerous pictures to refer back to as I wrote my books, and so I took a picture of those stairs. When I saw it on my computer screen, there was a distinct white, hazy, human-shaped figure halfway up the stairs. Many people noted it when it was posted on social media.

Finally, there is the event that motivated one of the stories in this book. My husband and I stayed at the Roubidoux (pronounced ROO-bi-doo) Campground in Waynesville, Missouri when we went to see my son graduate from Fort Leonard Wood. Having discovered a wonderful, almost magical glade and pool on a walk earlier in the day, I took my husband back there that evening. We started in full light but evening fell fast. *Very* fast! Dusk was growing deeper as we sat on a rock at the side of the pool talking. Suddenly, I heard a sound in the woods behind us.

I freely admit I have a big imagination. (What writer doesn't?) But there had been no sound of anything approaching—only suddenly a sound a mere few feet behind us. Regardless of whether it was an animal or a person (and the sound was such that it would have been a man or a large animal), we got up to leave, crossing a boardwalk that edged around the pool to the other side.

On the other side of the pool, my husband looked back to where we had been sitting. He saw in the trees, just feet behind where we had been, a tall, upright figure that he could only describe as inky, oily blackness. It was the size of a man but not quite the right shape, the 'head' not being big enough.

We both felt a strong sense of *Leave* from whatever it was but my husband, in particular, felt deeper senses of malice, even evil, coming from where it stood in the trees.

If this was a ghost, we concluded, it stood to reason something bad had happened there. Rarely, if ever, do we hear of hauntings where someone died a happy, joyful death. We knew from the many historical signs around Waynesville that the Trail of Tears passed through this town. On further research, it seemed highly likely that the Cherokee people had almost certainly camped beside that pool.

We began to research, questioning what might have happened at that particular spot that left an entity filled with malice and anger. We came up with two very different stories.

This collection is not merely about the strange and inexplicable. It's about the stories we believe and the things we fear and *why* we believe and fear. It's about how we live our lives and what we leave behind.

Trail of Tears

I am here
They call it the Trail of Tears.

Agilisi is old and weak as we come to the water.
"Rubie-doo," the soldiers shout. And, "Waynesville."

On March 12, 1839, we come to the water's edge.

It is not wide. It is not terribly deep—except to the young and to the old. To the weak and infirm. To the heavy wagons. I tell grandmother to stay and I slide through the huddled groups and the soldiers, through old men clustered together and young mothers wrapping babes tight to their chest, trying to keep them warm.

The water is of the deepest, swirling blue. The wooded glade is beautiful with towering pines.

Our chief speaks with the white man with long, drooping hair under his nose. I feel the tension between them.

Who wins, I do not know. But our chief speaks to the elders who move through our people and I see them begin to settle, to make beds for themselves and pull out small pots. Fires are built. Young men wade into the cold water, seeking fish. Soldiers heft rifles to shoulders and head into the woods.

I weave through the throngs back to Agilisi.

I am all she has left. Her son, my father, died two winters ago, shot by a soldier.

My mother and infant brother died fifty miles back, too weak to continue. We do not have enough food. Those of us who live are thin as specters.

I find Agilisi crouched by the water's edge, swirling her wrinkled fingers in the teal blue water.

The sun is fading above.

"A place of power," she whispers. "Do you feel it?"

I crouch down beside her, watching for a moment the bubbling of a spring from beneath the water, rippling the blue surface like a dance.

I close my eyes and wait, seeking in the air around me, listening beyond the rustle and footsteps of a thousand feet of Cherokee and soldiers, beyond the smell of campfires beginning.

They say I am gifted with the Sight, as my father was, as Agilisi is. Behind my closed eyelids, I see a vision.

It is a sunny day. A family sits by the pool. I see little of them but that they are a family. A girl sits on a bridge above it. Two dogs dash in and out of the water. They are happy and unaware of me.

The day is theirs, Agilisi whispers. *One day there will be no more tears here, but happiness. Come.*

I open my eyes, looking to her. Has she seen the same?

She rises and I, beside her. We go but twenty steps into the wood. Agilisi's old friend beckons us to join her at the fire her son has started. I squat beside it, looking back to the pool, to where the spring bubbles.

The day fades into evening, dark falling quickly. A strange

people walk at the pool's edge, seeming to pass through the Cherokee and soldiers who also mill there. A white man wears *ashulohi*. But strange ones. They end at his knees, showing his bare legs beneath. He wears a shirt covered in flowers.

He walks with a woman odder still. She wears a tunic, not so different from my own that falls to my mid-thigh, but that hers is thin, black, a sheen to it. Night is falling quickly. It is her legs that are unlike anything I've ever seen. Are they even human? They are like an animal's legs, sleek and patterned in black and white. I strain forward. They shine like snakeskin or perhaps like the sleek fur on a horse's legs after rain.

I watch them at length.

They talk softly, smiling and laughing. He kisses her, embraces her, runs his hand the length of long, golden hair falling down her back. They sway together for a moment and pull apart, laughing.

One day there will be happiness here, Agilisi whispers again. She sighs and lays down on her blanket. A shiver comes over her. "I will not go from here," she says. "Bury me and let my resting place be a place of joy by day. But grant my bones rest by night."

She sighs, a deep breath, and her thin chest is still.

"No," I whisper.

Her friend presses her hand to Agilisi's eyes, closing the lids. "Sleep well, Old Friend," she says. "We will meet soon."

Her son stands up. I jolt to my feet, three steps to one side— *Agilisi is gone!*—three steps back. *She was all I had left.*

"No!" The word comes from my throat.

The woman in the black tunic, with the strange legs, turns her head sharply, peering into the forest. She looks right at me.

But there is no sign of recognition on her face. I believe she does not see me.

She rises to her feet, sounding fearful. "Something moved in the woods," she says.

I hear her words clearly.

Let my resting place be a place of joy.

They were happy here. The woman takes the man's hand and hastens over the water, to the other side of the pool.

Already, the soldiers are coming. Major Foster is at their forefront. He bows his head before me, taking my hand between his. He has often slipped extra food to Agilisi. I know it was from his own rations. I've watched him grow nearly as gaunt as we, the Cherokee do.

There is grief in his blue eyes. "I'm sorry. I'm so sorry."

I do not understand Foster. He forces us from our homes, yet he shows us kindness. His grief seems genuine.

I yank my hands from his, saying coldly, "We will bury her. The night is ours. It is time for you to go." I walk, three paces to one side, three paces to another, and look to the strange couple in the forest.

"It is time for you to go," I say to the soldier, but my eyes are locked on the strange man and woman. "You do not belong here.

The man looks back.

Unlike the woman—he sees me.

His eyes sink into mine.

I sense his fear and I smile, slowly.

Let my resting place be a place of joy.

It will be, Agilisi, I promise. By day it will be. But by night, this will be your resting place and they will not disturb you. The night is ours.

The couple turns and hurries down the dark path, with only the barest of moonlight showing above.

Life will go on—but here, in this spot, perhaps on Cherokee terms.

For I am here.
On the Trail of Tears.

Helga the Horrible

In a land far away, or so I was told, lived Helga the Horrible, a hideous creature whose evil deeds were whispered throughout the land. From the time I was a boy at the castle of Drogunfell, I remember Radiant Roselle telling of Helga's evil deeds, as we sat around the hearth after the evening meal. The light flickered from the dancing flames over Roselle's golden hair as she plaited reeds into mats for the floor, and told how Helga had hunted her, chasing her down.

It was true, my older brothers assured me. Don't go in the forest! Don't go near her hut! She'll try to lure you in with questions, with bribes, perhaps sweet treats!

And there was the time, Kendrick told me, that Horrible Helga took Radiant Roselle's little daughter, lovely Tia, only eleven at the time, and rode away with her into the woods, refusing to bring her back. Tia, brushing her long golden hair by the fire, nodded solemnly. Uncle Airhorn must have rescued her, I thought, for here she was.

I confess—the story captivated me. As I sat by

the fire, as I lay in bed at night or went to the chapel every morning, the story would play out in my mind.

Uncle Airhorn, big and strong, with triangular patches of beard on his jaw and chin that marked him as the supreme lord of the castle, a man no other dared challenge, rode out on his great steed, his arrow and sword, his spear and knife, to hand, braving the Fearsome Forest where evil things dwelt, in search of Lovely Tia. Through the darkness he rode, cleverly evading the night serpents that fell from the trees above and the Lurking Lorcas that waded in the creek's waters, hoping to spring on the flesh of an unsuspecting traveler. Surely he fought the Giant Java on his way, and emerged, finally, into the dark clearing where stood Horrible Helga's hut.

Airhorn was not deterred by the awful sight—walls made from the bones of his predecessors, the windows framed in with the broken teeth of those who had challenged Helga and curtains made of the flapping skin of unfortunate travelers. No, Airhorn rode into the clearing, fearless, and shouting, "My daughter, Horrible Helga! Bring her out now or you die!"

Did a mighty battle ensue? Did Helga defend her prize with all her strength and wiles?

I see Airhorn swoop in, his sword flying against Helga's spells. The massive wart on her nose is no deterrent to him. He laughs as she points her wicked wand and flings his sword up at her owl bearing down on him with beating wings and vicious yellow eyes alight with the lust for blood! Airhorn sends an arrow arcing through the morning sky. It slices off tail feathers and the owl spins helplessly, plummeting to earth!

She calls her Giant Java but Airhorn's on it, his sword flashing, slicing, chopping, dicing, till the vicious creature lies dead at his feet. Lovely Tia wails in distress, her golden hair caught in the witch's hand as Helga laughs and laughs, and sends her Night Serpents at him. Three! Four! They drop from the trees, entangling him, twisting around his ankles, his waist.

"Papa! Papa!" shrieks Lovely Tia, her golden hair still twisted in the clutch of Horrible Helga.

Airhorn has a knife in each hand. They flash silver in the morning light, catching a serpent in its mouth, between its fangs; stabbing another in the abdomen. He stomps on the tail of a third and ties it in a knot around the trunk of a tree where it thrashes helplessly. The fourth is gutted! And he laughs as Helga steps back in fear.

"Never touch my daughter again!" His voice rings out in the clearing till the bones that form her walls shudder and rattle.

He swings Lovely Tia up on the saddle behind him, her golden hair swinging out in a brilliant arc. She sticks her tongue out at Horrible Helga, and Airhorn rides, *rides!* through the Fearsome Forest, now aiming an arrow, now swinging a sword, now flashing a knife at a forest creature, until his mighty steed gallops from the forest line, breaking onto the wide palace lawn, and skids to a halt, leaving dark tracks of upturned dirt in the fresh green grass.

And Lovely Tia slides to the lawn, the young squires rushing to take her hands, to lead her to the castle, each hoping for her favor. She graces each and every one with a smile. Her mystique increases, year by year, as the tale of her harrowing capture and escape spreads.

And every night, she brushes her long golden hair by the fire, as the young squires look on, each hoping she'll once again favor him with a smile—and perhaps, if the stories whispered in the barns and armory are true—just a bit more.

I watched in awe as Radiant Rosella plaited reeds by the light of the fire, and Lovely Tia combed her golden locks and at a table, Airhorn sharpened his knives and drank his ale, his eyes lighting on his radiant wife and lovely daughter. The people of the castle stayed close within its walls, or went only west to the village on market days The women warned us children of the Fearsome Forest and the dangers that lurked there and sometimes all eyes would turn to lovely Tia and she would nod solemnly: It was all true. She alone of all of us had been there, had seen it.

The years passed and I joined the squires, learning to sharpen the weapons and groom the horses; to fight against the pell and help Airhorn into his armor.

The squires and lads were all in awe of Airhorn. He strutted through the castle courtyard, lord of his manor, and all the boys wanted to be him. Lovely Tia sashayed with one lad after another in the castle gardens, holding hands and fluttering eyelashes, while Airhorn scowled and told her she was too young and Ravishing Rosella plaited reeds with the flickering flames lighting her golden locks, and rolled her eyes and said, "Lovely Tia, they are *not* your boyfriends! You are much too young!"

But Lovely Tia knew they were. She knew she was ravishing. And as she grew, ready to greet and choose among the many suitors sent from other castles, she only knew it more and more.

Then one day, shortly after I'd been knighted, it happened: A massive stag fled into the Fearsome Forest! Airhorn swore as he and his men marched into the great hall. He had no time for pursuing the beast. He had important meetings with his councilors. "Who will get this stag for me!" he demanded.

With a fantasy of winning Lovely Tia's attention, who even now sat by the fire, I shot to my feet. "I will, my lord!"

"Good lad!" he bellowed.

Lovely Tia smiled at me. My knees felt weak!

I nervously strapped my knives to my boots and forearms; my sword to my side and my bow and quiver to my back. I re-lived every memory of Airhorn fighting the Night Serpents and the Giant Java, those many years ago, and swallowed hard, assuring myself I could do it, too.

Airhorn strutted forth from the Great Hall as my own squire cinched the girth on my steed's saddle. "The Giant Java, my lord..." I began. "If it attacks...."

He stared at me a moment, the triangular patches of beard black against his white skin. "The Giant Java?"

"The hideous beast with the hairy head," I reminded him. "If it attacks...."

He threw his head back, laughter filling the courtyard. "There is no Giant Java!" he said. "Who told you these fairy tales?"

I swallowed. My memory said the Ravishing Rosella had whispered of the Giant Java around the flickering flames, the nights she told of the Lovely Tia being heisted away by Horrible Helga. My mind flickered, like those long-ago flames, to those long-ago years. Had Ravishing Rosella ever actually told the story of that great battle to rescue Lovely Tia? I was suddenly not sure. Surely I had not conjured up the Giant Java out of nowhere?

"I spoke in jest," I assured Lord Airhorn. I forced out a laugh to prove that I spoke true and surely I convinced him, for he lifted his chin, with its triangles of beard, to the sky, blue above the castle courtyard, and laughed with me. "Bring back the stag," he said.

And the gears ground loudly and the portcullis rose slowly. Lovely Tia stood in the courtyard, her golden hair flowing to her waist and shining in the sun, and she blew me a kiss. Squire Oran pressed close to her and she looked up to him, her eyelids batting and her red lips curving up. Oh, Tia was lovely! I touched spurs to horse and trotted out into the Great Beyond, across the emerald green lawn that surrounded the palace, followed by my squires, their hearts surely pounding as mine did, to face that Fearsome Forest where once Lovely Tia was held captive among the Night Serpents and Lurking Lorcas. Even without the Giant Javas—mythical though they turned out to be—my insides crawled with the anticipation of meeting the rest.

But to win Lovely Tia's admiration—I would gladly face

them!

My horse ambled across the wide lawn beyond the castle, through the forest glade, and down a dappled forest path, where birds twittered and called, while behind me my men rode.

I thought of that long-ago story, of Lovely Tia, in her childhood, dragged down the forest path by her golden hair. How fearful she must have been! And what a lovely young woman she had become, I thought. Never once had she shown any sign of the trauma of that time! My gaze drifted upward to the limbs cloistering above us, full of leafy green. I scoured their peaceful presence for any sign of the Night Serpents.

I saw none. But then, it wasn't night We would find the stag long before dusk and be gone, I told myself as our horses trotted down the dappled path, with patches of sunlight caressing and sliding across their chestnut withers. Birds chirped, unseen, in the trees above and now and again one swooped down and back up in a flash of red or green or blue. It was hard to believe such evil dwelt in such a beautiful place. I glanced back at my men—boys, really: Oran, Owen, and Alan. Fear flickered across their faces

Suddenly, Oran screamed—yes, a high-pitched scream—and pointed to the trees above. At first, I saw nothing

Then Owen, too, pointed, shouting, "It's the Giant Java!"

And there it was, staring back at me, a massive furred creature, hanging upside down from a branch. My heart pounded. Why had Airhorn said they didn't exist!

Oran, Owen, and Alan bolted, whirling their horses, kicking their heels in and shouting, "Hiya!"

My heart beat wildly; my hand went to my sword. I thought of Lovely Tia waiting; seeing Oran racing back in shame. I almost smiled. Surely her heart would turn to he who returned having been brave enough, as her father had been, to face the Giant Java for her.

I had a moment of doubt. Oran, at least, *would* return. It would be a mite difficult to win her love as a mutilated corpse.

My hand clutched more tightly to my sword.

The Giant Java gazed at me from eyes ringed in a dark mask. I realized it wasn't moving.

It blinked, let out a sigh, and closed its eyes.

I let out my own breath. My shoulders relaxed. I studied it a bit more. It was of enormous size, as big as a man, but bulkier, with heavy arms covered in long fur. It must be the Giant Java. What else could it be? I waited what seemed a long time, knowing the stag might be getting further away, yet fearing to turn my back on the creature and fearing to go deeper into the forest, knowing, now, that Airhorn was wrong. The Giant Java existed—and presumably there were more of them.

At last it opened its eyes. It stared at me languidly, one might even say with curiosity—except it seemed not to have enough enough energy to muster up such an emotion. At last, I turned my horse and went deeper into the forest, assured the creature had no interest in harming me.

I listened intently for any sound of the stag. Far away in the forest, I heard the rustle of leaves, the burble of running water. Far away, I heard what might have been the call of the stag. I followed the dappled path, as the sun grew warm. At last I came to a stream, where I dismounted, and knelt to cup my hands and drink cool water. I took bread and cheese from the pouch at my waist and ate in the quiet glade.

I kept my sword close, wary of other Giant Javas—perhaps the one I saw was old and sick and others would not be so placid —and for Night Serpents and Lurking Lorcas. I realized I didn't even know what a Lorcas was. How would I know if I saw one? It would be vicious, I decided. It would lurk behind a tree, peer out, and suddenly attack.

It was at that moment I saw bright eyes peering at me from amidst the ferns clustered at the bottom of a tree barely a sword's length from me. I scrambled to my feet. It was lurking! I snatched up my sword—but the thing dashed away, the size of a small dog, with red fur.

It was clearly more fearful of me than I was of it. I half lowered the sword. It might not have been the Lurking Lorcas. Maybe the lurking Lorcas was *large*. Maybe it was larger than the Giant Java.

It came from the water, I remembered, and uneasily mounted my steed, backing him away from the water's edge, up to the path. The trail, however, ran beside the stream. Unable to get away from it, I kept a wary eye on the water.

And then! The sound of an infant crying! From the water! What man could run from such a sound, no matter the danger to himself! I threw myself to the ground, sword to hand, and raced for the bank, scanning the water, the shores, for the infant in distress. The Lurking Lorcas was surely preparing to devour the poor creature.

The cry stopped. Two tiny, dark, beady eyes peered at me from across the little stream. I fought the urge to back away, but stepped into the water, prepared to fight—if only I could find the infant!

The baby wailed again, followed by, "Maaaa! Maaaa!" Then I saw the head just rising above the water's surface, and the creature's back. It seemed long and narrow, coming straight at me. Two more followed it. Still, there was no sign of a child.

I backed away, backed up to my horse: and watched as three furry animals—a mother and her babies by all appearances—with ridiculous, short legs waddled up on the shore, dragging flat tails behind them. The big creature looked at me, uttered, "Maaa, maaa!" and disappeared into the foliage. Her babies let out wails like an infant crying, and a moment later, I saw them, farther down the bank, slide back into the water.

Slowly, my heart stopped its hammering.

I glanced at the sun. I'd now been in the forest at least two marks of the sundial and so far nothing had attacked me. The thought flashed across my mind: Had Lovely Tia or the Ravishing Roselle possibly exaggerated the story?

It flashed away as quickly. I'd heard the tale for years. It was merely that I was not yet in the Forest Deep. Down the path, I heard the call of the stag. I vaulted back onto my fine horse and kicked his sides. I must hurry if I were to find the stag and get out before nightfall!

The beast seemed to taunt me. Always just out of reach, it lured me deeper and deeper. The path narrowed and the canopy of leaves grew closer together, far above my head. I eyed the tree limbs far above. The Night Serpents must surely think it night!

I tried to watch for them even as I sought the stag, listening for it, scanning the path and the trees for it—and thinking the whole time how pleased Lovely Tia would be when I brought it home! I glanced again at the cover of leaves above that dimmed the forest here below, and wondered how I would judge the passing of time. There must be sun, still, for it was dim—a deep green shady sort of cool dim—rather than dark. But I began to think that I must turn and head home, lest I be caught for the night.

The stag called one more time. I hesitated, looking up to the leaves. They seemed to grow darker even as I watched and the air around me seemed to cool.

Reluctantly—yet with my heart once again taking up its hammering at the thought of night falling in the Fearsome Forest —I turned my horse's head. He stopped in the path.

And I saw it: a thick-bodied black serpent stretched the width of the trail.

The horse backed up a step. I yanked my bow from my back.

"Tchuss, tchuss, don't shoot it."

My head spun at the voice. A small old woman stood in the path, her skin pale and smooth, despite her obvious age; her cheeks round as apples. She held a lantern, smiling at me from its glow

"'Tis already gone," she said.

I hated to take my eyes off her—it could only be Helga the Horrible! But I had no choice. And sure, she was right! The path was bare. I looked back to her—the fearsome old witch who had haunted my childhood! If I galloped, would she send her owl after me?

"They're more fearful of you," she said, "than you are of them. Unless you step on them by accident, they'll run from you."

Still I said nothing. I looked down the path.

Helga shook her head—for it must be Helga. "I'm thinking you'd not be wanting to try for home tonight." She lifted her lantern, and her eyes, toward the tangled branches above. They were dark and when I returned my gaze to her, I realized how the path itself had become even dimmer.

"'Twill take a good two hours to reach the castle," Helga said and I thought she sounded amused, in addition to sounding quite reasonable. In fact, she sounded much as the nanny at the castle did when speaking to silly children.

My eyes narrowed. She was *laughing* at me. And yet, as I contemplated her peaceful smile, it seemed it was not a cruel laugh.

"Surely they teach language at the castle?" she said. Her smile grew. "I find it hard to think that Airhorn would have a mute as one of his men, so you must be able to speak." Again, she sounded amused.

"I speak quite well," I informed her. I reminded myself not to be taken in by appearances. She *had,* after all, fought a mighty battle against Airhorn and abducted the Lovely Tia. "It is merely that I have nothing to say to you. I shall go home tonight regardless."

"Aye, well, you shall try," she returned. The lantern now showed only her face in its small circle of light. Behind her, all was bathed in the black of a tarry night.

"Surely you are not threatening me!" I declared. "I am a knight in the service of Lord Airhorn who has already defeated you!"

Helga chuckled. "I suppose he has at that. No, 'tis not I who would prevent you, but the night. You may remember from your ride in that the path twists a great deal. It rises and falls, sometimes abruptly. In the dark, even with a lantern, 'tis a dangerous place to ride, where a horse or man might easily stumble and twist an ankle or walk into a thicket or tree or get turned around and lost."

I considered my options. She seemed to read my mind.

"You cannot try for home in this darkness," she said. "You *could* sleep here on the path and wait for morning, but I do have a bed and a hot soup on the hearth. While I haven't a fine castle, I daresay what I have is clean and far more comfortable than sleeping on the road."

I weighed the thought of waking up with an adder looking in my face to the question of what I might find in her abode.

In the lantern light, her face took on an eerie glow. "Come now," she said, and I thought a note of impatience had crept into her voice. "I offer you a clean bed, a warm hearth, and a full stomach. I can assure you my hut is not made of the bones of your predecessors." She laughed. "But I'll not stand out all night waiting for you to decide whether to believe fairy tales."

She turned and disappeared into the trees.

Black night quenched my senses, so thick it pressed on my open eyes as if they were squeezed tight. I jumped from my horse and led it, hurrying, after the pin-prick of light. My hammering heart had made the decision.

"There is no eye of newt in my stew, I promise you," she said.

"I do not believe fairy stories," I said haughtily, trying to maintain my dignity. But I couldn't stop my curiosity. "If your shack is not made of bones, how did you know they say so in the castle?"

I could just make out her form, a dark silhouette edged by the glow of the lantern in front of her, against the dark night. The horse rustled behind me, its nose nearly on my ear. I could feel its fear. It had been trained for war—not for this oppressive darkness.

"My dear granddaughter told me, last time I visited her, that she would tell the whole castle such a tale." The woman sighed. "She was quite angry."

"Had she not a right to be, when you kidnapped her and fought her father?" I demanded. Even in this darkness, I could still see Lovely Tia sitting by the fire, stroking her long golden hair with the boar bristle brush.

"Let us eat," Helga said with a sigh. She lifted the lantern higher and now I saw, in the distance, a faint glow of yellow and orange. As we drew closer, I could see it was the flames of a hearth, showing through a glass-paned window. My heart surged with joy to see light!

"Your horse can stay in the stable." As we stepped into the soft glow around the hut, Helga indicated a little stable, not six *pieds* from the hut. "'Tis full with clean hay and food," she said. "Come in when you've cared for the animal, and I'll dish up stew."

I looked from her and the cottage into which she disappeared to the stable. I would be able to see the light. I really had no choice, I thought. It did cross my mind to sleep in the stable with my fine steed, but the smell of roasting meat and fresh vegetables and a hearty roast came easily to me in the night. My stomach rumbled.

Mind games, tricks, spells, I warned myself.

I took the animal into the stable and as she had promised, it had stalls—two of them, one with a horse in it already—full of clean hay.

I removed my beast's saddle, and used the equipment on the wall to care for it, before leading it into the second stall. The aroma of roasting meat seemed to grow stronger. *It could be human flesh*, I warned myself.

Her horse whinnied at me. I patted its nose. It seemed happy and well-cared for. Could a witch really shower such love on a horse, yet eat children? Of course, I told myself. But the image of the smiling old woman with rosy cheeks made it hard to convince myself.

But then again—did evil not specialize in presenting the image of an angel of light?

The scent of the stew set my stomach to loud growling.

I went to the doorway of the stable, studying the cottage. The stable was so close that I could see, in what little light spilled through the window, that it seemed to be of stone, with a thatched roof. I thought I could see a large garden on one side of the path we'd followed to the front door, stretching away into darkness.

My stomach growled loudly, clenching in on itself, and the door of the little cottage opened. She stood there, waiting.

I could certainly handle an old woman, I decided—if she proved to be so deceptive and beguiling after all. I crossed the distance in a few paces and entered her home.

I looked to the windows. No broken teeth were in evidence. They were framed, rather, by smoothly polished wood. And the curtains, if I was not mistaken, were of white lace.

Helga caught my look and chuckled. "I hope you're not disappointed. 'Tis no human skin on my windows." She turned her back to me, leaning over a cauldron.

I stepped back, feeling my own foolishness, and yet still relieved to see that when she rose and turned, she held a bowl, filled to the top, with dark gravy and meat and carrots and onions, and set it on the table with a spoon, across from one already filled and waiting.

"Take your pick," she said with a wink. "So you'll not fear I've poisoned one."

I glared at her, but chose the one she'd just dished up. "Thank you," I muttered, and lifted the spoon, trying hard not to gobble.

But the seasonings were so rich, the meat so delectable, the carrots and onions bursting with flavor, that I soon found it easy to savor each bite.

I swallowed, my eyes wide, and the words slipped out. "How is it that food on this earth can taste so good!"

Helga shrugged. "Hunger does wonders for flavor."

She abruptly set her spoon in her bowl. "I've not introduced myself. My name is Helen."

I stared at her, laying down my own spoon. "Helen?"

Again, the laugh. "What were you told?"

"Helga," I said.

"Helga. Hm." She pursed her lips a moment, staring at the ceiling, from which hung clusters of carrots and onions and leeks and a brace of hare before saying, "Aye, well, it does mean *blessed* and you can see I'm quite blessed with a very comfortable home and good food."

I glanced around the cottage. It did indeed look comfortable, with a well-cushioned chair by the window, and a basket of yarn beside the chair; rooms curtained off on either side, behind which, I guessed, must be the beds, and the fire roaring under the heavy pot of stew. I guessed that by day the lace curtains would be a pleasant and warm sight.

"You do know," she said pleasantly, "that it is I who should be afraid of you."

"Why would you fear me?" I asked, perplexed.

"You've grown up, if I'm not mistaken from your demeanor, on stories of the evil creature in the forest. Might you not decide to slay me in the night and return a hero?"

I felt my eyebrows furrow. No, I had not considered such a thing.

"I've no defense against a strong young knight who is twice my size."

I glanced at the bowl.

"Tchuss! There's no poison there. If I wanted to poison you, what would be the sense in using a potion that made me wait for it to act? I'd rather bury the body sooner than later."

I cleared my throat. "They say you have a wand and an owl."

"I've no wand. Unless Tia meant my stirring spoon." She nodded at the large handle sticking out from the cauldron. "Certainly you find my cooking near magical." She flashed a smile. "But no, I've no defense against you a'tall."

"Then why did you bring me in?" I asked. "You could have left me in the forest."

"'Tis not who I am," she said softly.

"How did you know I was there?" I asked suspiciously, thinking of the long walk to her cottage.

"You are a blunderbuss," she said good-naturedly. "I could hear you from furlongs away. Also, Jenna in the stable became restless. Further, the trail from the forest path to my home is really quite short. It only seems long in the dark of night, when you do not know where you're going and are afraid."

"I was not afraid!" I protested stiffly.

Helen smiled and reached across the table to pat my hand, taking me by surprise. I yanked it back. Her touch was warm, her palm soft. I had yet to see a wart on her nose and her finger nails were not the claws I'd been told.

"Tell me," she said, "How is my granddaughter? I know she's well-cared for, of course. But how *is* she?"

I stared stupidly, unsure how to answer such a question.

"She is much admired...." I stopped. Was I to tell this old woman that all the young men of the castle craved Lovely Tia's affections? And perhaps not in the purest way. It seemed suddenly tawdry to speak of to an old woman, to a grandmother who seemed, in the flickering flames, to speak with love of her granddaughter.

"She *is* lovely," Helen said.

I studied Helen's face and thought that perhaps in her youth she had been quite lovely herself. Might Tia have gotten it from her? I noted that her hair, though white and coiled on her head in braids, must be quite long and quite thick.

"Is she admired for her wisdom, her learning, her charity, her heart?"

"I...I believe she...um...reads...now and again." I stumbled in my words. "Sometimes."

Helen leaned forward, her eyes opening wider. "Tell me what books she likes!" She glanced at a wall of the cabin and I saw it was lined with a hundred books or more.

I frowned, trying to remember the last time I had seen Tia read. It had been many months ago, during a vicious winter storm. Ravishing Roselle told her to sit and read for a spell. Tia had pouted at the book handed her, rolled her eyes, and after a page or two, cast it aside with a huff.

"Well, I couldn't say—for sure. That is to say, I don't know what her favorites are."

Helen deflated a little. She lifted another spoon of stew to her mouth. I suspected she hoped for me to answer that Tia was admired for wisdom, charity, heart. I couldn't think of a time anyone had sought Tia's wisdom. No, the young men were entranced by her hair, her lovely blue eyes, and her fair fetching face and the young women of the castle found it to their benefit to befriend the lord's daughter.

I had, in fact, once heard Brunella and Browanda whispering outside the stable, laughing at Lovely Tia's airs. "What has she to lift her nose about," Brunella had said. "The little twit doesn't even know the horses must have their saddles removed after the hunt."

"She's never had to do it for herself," Browanda replied. "Or anything else, for that matter."

"Is she...at least...happy?" Helen asked hopefully.

"She wants for nothing," I answered.

"Yes, of course. But is she *happy*?"

As if a window pane had been scrubbed, I abruptly saw my

own yearnings for Tia in ugly clarity. Didn't I want a woman of wisdom, charity, and heart?

I stood abruptly from the table. "No," I said angrily. "No, she is not happy. She sits by the fire and combs her hair endlessly and makes eyes at the squires and sets us all to fighting amongst ourselves and I believe she delights in doing so!"

Helen stared sadly into her stew. "I'm sorry," she said. "And I'm sorry I've upset you. But why? Why are you angry with your answer?"

"Because I'm angry at my own foolishness." The words spilled out. "How is it I've never seen this before? How is it you ask one question and the entire scene, all I've ever known, suddenly shifts before my very eyes and I see something in her I've never seen before?"

Helen touched my bowl, indicating that I should resume my seat and eat. I thumped myself down onto the bench. But I couldn't bring myself at the moment to take another spoonful.

"Because nobody has asked the question before," she said. "Nobody speaks in Drogunfell of happiness. They're not looking for it so they're not thinking of it and certainly not finding it."

She sounded so sad that I wished for a moment I had lied.

She heaved a sigh. "I hoped. But I see now I'd not have believed it anyway had you told me she was happy." She shook her head. "No, the traits of a lifetime do not change in a few short years."

I glanced at her, and around the cottage full of fresh food and yarn and lace curtains and books and a warm fire, and took a hasty gulp of the still-hot stew.

"But you kidnapped her."

"Ah, now, that depends how you define kidnap." Helen grinned.

Her quick change of mood lightened my own and I found myself smiling back, though my mind screamed that I was being sucked in to the old witch's lies. But she had me curious.

"How *do* you define it?" I asked.

She smiled. "I asked Roselle if I might take her to my cottage. I hoped she might like to care for the horse and tend the garden. 'Tis *good* for children to create, to care for, to grow—to watch the fruits of their own labor and see they can make goodness grow from the earth or feel the love of the horse they've just fed."

"Roselle *allowed* you?" I asked. I could feel the hard edge in my voice. No matter how good her intentions, it was still abduction if she'd not been given permission. And I'd heard the story over and over.

"Oh she did indeed. Tia and I set out into the forest and after a bit, she protested that the way was too long. She wanted to turn back. By this time, however, we were nearly to my cottage and the stew had been on the hearth. It needed looking to, as did the goats. I told her we'd be here anon, that we would have a bite to eat, feed the goats and chickens and rabbits, and I'd bring her home if she still wished."

I leaned in. The firelight played over her coils of white hair and her fine, soft skin.

"She protested greatly," Helen said. "But we were only minutes from the trail. As we reached the cottage, she demanded we turn around. I said I would have a bite myself, for I am old and cannot ride hours without food, and feed the animals and we should go. I had just come inside to stir the stew when I turned and saw her kick poor Jenna in the leg, and run back down the trail, shouting at the top of her lungs for her father."

"He was surely nowhere near?" I asked.

"Oh, aye, he was out in the woods hunting that day. But she'd certainly no notion of how to get home and nor did I think she'd be wary of the adders, and perhaps in her anger kick at one of them and get bitten."

The fire was dying.

"I hastened after her, with the spoon still in my hand, shouting for her to watch for adders, and that she didn't know the way and would get lost."

"How far did she get?" I imagined eleven year old Tia in the wood. I thought that Helen's story was certainly believable. I had, in truth, seen her kick the castle dogs when she was younger— and even in recent years.

"Far enough I was winded when I saw what I had feared—the adder stretched across the path. I yelled in warning, just as my son came down the path, galloping for her. He, too, saw, the adder and threw a knife as it raised its head to strike."

So that part was true, I thought. I confess I thought it a bit smugly. Airhorn *had* killed a Night Serpent with a knife! He was such a warrior as to ride a steed at full speed and still strike a serpent with a flying knife!

"He did get it?" I clarified.

Helen shook her head. "No, he missed and it bit her."

My last hope flagged. "Was *none* of it true?" I demanded. "What happened after she was bitten?"

"I've plenty of marigold in my garden. He carried her back and we treated it. They're not *highly* venomous. He raged and railed that I should have turned immediately when she told me to and he put her on the back of his horse and rode away."

I slapped my spoon into my now empty bowl. I guess I got one crumb. That he put her on the back of his horse and rode away was true.

Helen reached across the table and again patted my hand. This time, I let her. She was comforting me? *She* was comforting *me*. And still, my mind protested—maybe she was lying. Maybe she would kill me while I slept.

"I've not seen her since that day," Helen said with a sigh. "She was such a sweet little girl. She used to love coming here and putting her hands in the dirt and feeding the chickens and seeing flowers and vegetables come up where she planted seeds.

"And slowly, she changed."

She shook her head abruptly, the heavy coils of white hair

swaying, and cleared the bowls away to a small pot full of water by the hearth. "Ah, well, we can but pray, aye? I told you only because you asked. I offered you a place to sleep and food only because I'd not leave a man in such a dense and dark wood overnight, nor leave him hungry. Let us retire. She pointed to the door on the left of the cottage entrance. "That was Tia's room long ago." She winked at me suddenly. "I trust we will both still be alive in the morning?"

I couldn't help myself this time. I burst into laughter. "Helen —if that's your name—I promise not to kill the wicked witch of the Fearsome Forest if you promise not to kill a foolish dunderhead who believed fairy stories with no evidence!"

She patted my hand with a laugh and we parted ways, going to our separate rooms, each with a lantern.

I lifted mine high as I entered the little room where—if Helen was to be believed—Tia had slept. *If* Helen was to be believed— for years of hearing the stories had already crept back, asking me —was I *now* the dunderhead who believed foolishly? In her presence, it all sounded so reasonable.

I looked around the little room. Pink curtains fluttered faintly at the dark windows. A pink goose down blanket covered the big bed. Ah, well, I needn't tell the other knights, I thought wryly. I moved the lantern over the dressing table to see cards with pressed, dried flowers on them. Something was stuck in the mirror of the little dressing table and I took it out. It was one of the cards, with a dried impatiens pressed to it: The symbol of motherly love, a long ago memory whispered. *I love you Grandmama*, was scrawled on the paper in childish handwriting.

I dropped to the bed to remove my boots and leather armor, and climbed under the pink covers before blowing the lantern out. Well, I *had* always hoped to warm Tia's bed, I thought rather sardonically. I lay in the dense blackness. From outside came the contented murmur of the stream and I thought maybe I heard a chicken squawk once and settle down. The place felt safe and warm. I fancied I felt the love hovering in this very room. I drifted off to sleep and dreams of Helga the Horrible swinging an adder by the tail.

I jarred awake to a hideous screeching, and claws flailing in the gray light of early dawn, shrieking and claws coming at my eyes and feathers spinning around my face. I threw up my arms and rolled, falling out of Lovely Tia's bed and collapsing on the floor between the bed and window, scrambling to grab my knife.

And then Helga—or was it Helen?—collapsed across the pink-covered bed, clutching a large rooster who squawked angrily in her arms and shook his head in violent protest. She laughed until tears rolled down her cheeks, until the creature gave one last angry squawk and settled down.

"Are you done now," Helen demanded of it, carefully releasing her grip. The fowl shook its wings and seemed to give a *harumph* but settled into place in the middle of the pink bed.

In the morning light, Helen's skin seemed even more pink and fragile. Her hair, as long and thick as Tia's, hung down her back. Her eyes danced with happiness. "I forgot to warn you to shut the window! He likes to come in in the morning." She looked pointedly at the knife in my hand, still half raised. "I do hope you'll not kill him."

"He *would* make a good stew," I said.

I rode down the forest path in the bright morning light, my stomach full with eggs from the rooster's paramours—and the rooster himself still very much alive to carry on. I had helped Helen carry wood in to store beside her hearth. She was old—older than I'd realized in the dusk and firelight of the previous night. She needed help. I hauled in fresh hay to her stable and fed her horse and struck out on the road toward Drogunfell.

In the pouch at my waist I carried bread, cheese, and a small bunch of impatiens to give to Tia. The stag was all but forgotten.

Until—there it stood in my path.

I stared at it.

It stared at me.

Gripping the horse with my knees, I slowly pulled my bow from my back. The stag watched me nock an arrow, then turned its back to me and sauntered down the path.

I thought of Lovely Tia's eyes—the glow of admiration, the eyelashes that would bat and the fingers that would touch my leather armor—if I returned from a night in the Fearsome Forest with the stag dragging behind my horse.

I thought of Helen's eyes as she pressed the little cluster of impatiens into my hand: eyes so sad with loss.

I didn't need—I didn't *want*—Tia's admiration.

I lowered my bow.

Somehow, I think the stag knew I would.

Excerpt: The Water is Wide

Ireland and Scotland are reputed to have 'thin places': places where the veil is lifted between times, between worlds. There are stories throughout history of people disappearing into other times, of time slips in which people seem to witness and touch other times. This excerpt is based on this idea —that two times can overlap.

Scotland, Present

"It's a boy, Amy!" Angus brushes hair off my temple, whispering in awe as if I've single-handedly built mesas and splashed sunrise over the desert.

"A boy?" My heart pounds. I shake my head, denying.

"He's beautiful," Carol gushes.

Angus lays my son, bare and pink, on my chest. Carol gazes down at the tiny face with joy—the first real happiness she's had since Shawn's disappearance. I touch his hair, thick and black like mine. He struggles to gaze up at me. It's Shawn's face, looking up with dark, curious eyes. He blinks sleepily. His eyelids droop shut. He gives a little shuddering sigh and relaxes against my shoulder. Tears sting my eyes. He doesn't even know what trust is, yet he trusts he is safe in my arms, that I will protect him.

I close my eyes in prayer that I can. If this blessing means anything, if Shawn and Niall are related—and they must be, despite the mysterious James Angus who should have been the connection—then he's in danger. I need to go back to the States, to safety. But I can't leave Angus. I can't abandon Shawn in a brutal era. I can't leave myself to explain one day to my son why I abandoned his father. Will leaving the crucifix in a drawer protect him? Or is the blessing itself the real catalyst?

"What is his name?" Carol pulls me from my fears.

"James," I say without hesitation.

* * *

I wake from restless sleep, from dreams of the crucifix, of maces, swords and nooses; of filthy, sweaty, men in leather jerkins, frantic men pressed together under a mining cat, digging, digging, digging, as arrows hail down. My son is a child, on the field outside Carlisle, lost and scared amidst the battle. Shawn is there, under the mining cat. I'm reaching...reaching...reaching across time, unable to protect him, begging Shawn to save our son, but my voice is silent.

Still, something calls him. He turns. He sees the child. Unhesitating, he leaves the shelter of the cat; runs, hunched over. A bullish English soldier, with a large, black beard, turns toward James. An arrow streaks across the wet sky. A man bellows.

I jolt upright, breathing hard! The crucifix lies on my chest. The window shows the deep cobalt sky of pre-dawn.

"Sh, now." Angus sits, squeezed on the narrow hospital bed, beside me. He brushes my hair from my sweaty temple. "What is it?"

I see Shawn frozen in motion, reaching for a child he doesn't know is his. "It seems wrong that Shawn doesn't even know he has a son."

He strokes my hand, his face thoughtful. "Aye, it does, at that."

Glenmirril, 1315

Niall stood on the third floor, looking down through the arched window into Glenmirril's courtyard. The torrential downpour of the morning had given way to a weak stream of winter sunshine.

Darnley rode in, his horse splashing sparkling droplets of water from a puddle. He lifted a hand in greeting to MacDonald, and shouted something to the men behind him. They guffawed.

Niall wanted to be there, with his men, where he belonged. Instead, it was Shawn, who still had the longer hair the castle folk expected of Niall, who moved among the men, patting ponies, shouting orders to stable boys, directing the chaos as if born to it. He yelled and pointed, and Taran scrambled up the wooden stairs into the great hall.

A hand fell on Niall's sleeve. He jumped, grabbing quickly for the hood.

"'Tis but me," Allene said softly.

He turned away, wishing she would have stayed in their chambers, rather than catch him watching covertly. There were twenty-five men in the courtyard now. He scanned the crowd below, and found two more.

She took his stiff arm and pulled it around her waist.

Footsteps sounded on the stair, hurried and light. Niall and Allene sprang apart as Christina appeared at the top of the stairs, her face white.

"Christina!" Allene spoke in alarm. "What is amiss?"

Christina turned, pointing at the stairs. She moved her mouth, but no words came out. She stumbled, her hand falling on the handle of the door into Niall's chambers, and stood, staring back at the stairs.

Niall grabbed his dirk, throwing himself between Christina and whatever was coming. But the man who appeared at the top of the stairs made him catch his breath. His fingers went weak on the knife.

* * *

"Father!" Allene burst into the great hall. She ran through beams of sunlight pouring through high windows, turning the rushes on the floor to gold, and fell to her knees before the table, her eyes averted from the lords, whose faces would be heavy with disapproval at her interruption. Shawn rose from his seat. MacDonald laid a hand on his arm, and he lowered himself.

Allene gripped her father's hands. "Please, Father, please forgive me, but...*Niall*...his people are trying to reach him."

"His people?" demanded Lord Morrison. "What mean you?"

MacDonald and Shawn became still, but for their eyes meeting.

"She means naught," said the Laird. "She has been ill. Niall, escort your wife to your chambers. Immediately."

Only Shawn heard her whisper, "Thank you, Father. *Thank you.*"

Shawn hurried around the table, his cloak stirring the rushes. She gripped his arm, trying to appear ill, even as they wrestled over who would drag whom more quickly from the hall. With the door shut on the lords, she crushed his hand in hers, flying for the stairs, all pretense of illness abandoned, as he scrambled after her. She threw open the door of her chambers, slamming it behind them so quickly Shawn had to open it again and release his cloak.

Turning to the room, he saw none of the pandemonium he had

expected. The sun had broken from the clouds, skimming past a half-finished drawing on Christina's easel, and turning the room to a sunny, silver oasis of peace. Niall stood silently by the table, his arm around Christina's shoulder. Shawn stepped forward quickly, laying his hand on her other shoulder. Her face was bone white against her black hair, everything about her utterly still. "What is it?" he asked. "How can they...?"

"The window," Niall whispered.

Shawn raised his eyes to where they both stared. At first, he saw only a shimmer of light dancing through the panes of glass. "It's just...."

"No, look. Listen." Niall breathed out the words.

Shawn stepped forward, squinting, and caught his breath. He saw a man now, his own six feet, with a broad chest, ruddy cheeks and short black curls. He was hazy, ghost-like. "Why do you think he's my people?" he asked. "I've never seen him."

"His clothing." Niall didn't take his eyes from the man.

Then Shawn realized—twenty-first century clothing was still normal enough to him, it hadn't registered, despite months in tunics and cloaks and leather boots laced to his knees. The man wore a heavy blue peacoat.

"He's been calling your name."

"Shawn, are you here?" The man's deep, gruff voice held a heavy Scottish accent. Its modern sound fell strangely on Shawn's ears.

"He speaks English." Christina turned to him. Her fingers squeezed his arm. "Are you from England?"

"No." Shawn's eyes remained locked on the man. He stepped forward, directly before the hazy figure, and said, "I'm here. Can you hear me?"

The man made no response, but peered into the room. A frown flickered across his face, he muttered, and wrung a dark knit cap in his hands. "She had a boy!" The voice echoed as if down a long tunnel, but the words were clear.

Shawn's breath came hard and fast. "Amy," he whispered, and more loudly, "I'm here. Who are you?" *He had a son!*

The man glanced out the window, then studied one of the walls. "That's where the tapestry is, of you being chased by MacDougall," Shawn said to Niall. "Do you think he's looking at it?"

The man turned again. "She named him James, after your father."

Shawn squeezed his eyes shut, fighting the hot tears that pierced them. His heart tripped over a beat and sped up again. She'd remembered him! She'd honored his father.

"Shawn, she wants you to know," the man called.

"He's been saying it for ten minutes." Allene's fingertips fell on his forearm. Shawn's hand crept over hers, tightening.

The man returned to the window, gave his message again, and wandered across the room, drifting through the settee. Christina gasped. He stopped at the fireplace and spoke again. Shawn called to him several more times, with no response. Christina was still and white as a birch tree. Shawn put his arm around her. "It's okay. He's just giving me a message."

The shimmering shape walked through the door without opening it. They ran, heedless of two Nialls being seen, and threw open the heavy wooden door to stare after him, trailing misty silver through the gray stone hall. He shimmered and faded from sight.

The Garden

This story was inspired by two things. One was a very short story written more than forty years ago by one of my sister's friends which had a similar (though more gristly and tragic) outcome to this story.

The more immediate inspiration was a stay at a cabin on the North Shore where the owner, living in the cabin next door, made this story spring to mind. He was really quite a nice guy. This story could be perceived as very unfair to him. Who knows why people inspire stories about characters based on them, but who are actually nothing like them?

Danica waited impatiently in her Volvo outside the northern cabin. The owner was supposed to meet her here. She tapped red nails on the leather-laced steering wheel. She'd texted him 48 minutes ago that she'd be here in 45 minutes—and he was not yet pulling up the driveway to let her in. She wondered how long she'd have to wait. She had only a week off from her job at a TV station down in the Cities. She didn't want to spend that precious time sitting in a gravel driveway, waiting.

She got out of her car, scanning the grounds around the cabin —five acres, according to the Host Your Own website on which she'd found the property. A long gravel road led from a country highway up to the two-room cabin. Behind it and on the left grew a thick wood of fir, pine, and slender white birches. A stand of trees lined the driveway on the right. She marched into the grass there and saw behind the cabin a shell path leading across a long stretch of lawn to a lush garden that must have taken an acre or more on its own.

She followed the path to the garden gate, where she could see now the multitude of flowers—tiger lilies, roses of every hue, hydrangeas, lilacs, tulips, brown-eyed Susans, and at least a dozen more.

Danica opened the wrought iron gate and took a few steps in her new sandals, down the shell path, stopping between beds of bobbing tiger lilies. Farther down, she could see even more blooms—none of which she could name. She didn't really care. They were lovely and, she was sure, good for meditation and peace and really, in this hectic dog eat dog life of the news world, what else mattered?

"You're Danica?"

The deep voice jolted her from her thoughts.

Danica spun to see a man nearly a foot taller than herself, thirty-five years older—which must put him in his sixties—and as rotund as Santa Claus, with a beard to match. He even wore suspenders.

He held out his hand. "Carlton Lester."

"Yes, I'm Danica. I've been waiting for you." She glanced at the trees around the cabin and lack of car.

"I live next door," he said. He pointed and she could see,

through another stand of trees, a small house.

"It's a small cabin," he said, "but let me show you around."

No apology for being late, she thought, as he led her back down the path. They climbed the three stairs to the railed wooden deck that served as a porch, and he let her into the cabin. The tour was quickly concluded. What did it take to show a small kitchen, bedroom, bathroom, and sitting area with a kitchen table squeezed in between.

"The gardens are the real draw," Carlton said. "If you ever want to know what's in them...well, you have my phone number." He stared at her. "You remind me of a guest I had three years ago."

A chill shot up Danica's spine that spun itself quickly into irritation. Anger was always better than fear. "I'm sure we're all of a kind to you," she said. "Us city folks. The appliances work?"

Carlton smiled, beneath his full, white beard. "All's well. Don't be worried if you hear sounds outside your window at night. There are lots of critter in the forest around here."

Critter. Danica held back a laugh. Who used that word?

"Raccoon, deer, foxes, maybe a wolf or bear."

"Bear?" Danica smoothed a hand down her fitted jeans.

"Mainly nocturnal," Carlton said. "They won't bother you if you don't bother them."

"Mmm," Danica replied.

"There are some wonderful trails down by the river," Carlton added. "Not even the locals are aware of some of them. But every creek has one."

He droned on and on. Danica glanced at her Volvo, laden with her walking sticks and coolers of organic food and her two suitcases of layers for every possible weather—shorts and t-shirts and long sleeves and sweaters and leggings and jeans. Tennis shoes and sandals and hiking boots.

"She was so lovely." He suddenly interrupted himself. "Blond hair like yours. The prettiest name—Jacinta. A shame she never smiled. She was too rushed—never happy. Never took time to smell the flowers."

He seemed on the brink of saying more when a peal of thunder rumbled outside, saving her. "I should get things unloaded before the rain lets loose," she said.

"Some people are not as lovely on the inside as on the outside," Carlton said. "Unlike flowers. If you have time tomorrow, I'll show you the gardens. A beautiful place to relax and come back to what's important."

Danica turned for a moment toward the gardens, stretching far back toward the forests that backed up the property. They did seem exceptionally beautiful, beyond anything she'd ever seen. She dearly wanted him to *go*. She dreaded starting him on another long monologue, but curiosity suddenly filled her. "What's your secret?" she asked.

"Fertilizer." Carlton smiled. "Fertilizer that is not always believed to be the best." He laughed. "Manure sure stinks. But sometimes what is ugly sees itself and becomes greater."

Danica felt her eyebrows furrowing. *Uh, yeah, whatever that means,* she felt herself wanting to say. But she didn't really care. She was here for a week—not for a lifetime of platitudes.

"We should all try to make the world more beautiful," he added.

"I really have to get my things in." She didn't try to hide the irritation from her voice.

"Of course," he said.

Danica settled into the one-room cabin, pouring a glass of white wine after folding and laying out her clothes neatly atop the one table in the bedroom—there was no dresser. One star review for sure. She sat on the deck with the glass, enjoying the fire crackling in a tall smoke-stack fire pit.

She would work while she was here—yes—but it was a pleasant break from the city.

Her mind wove around the article she had to have in to Kevin by Saturday evening—tomorrow. She sipped her white wine, watching the fire, and thinking about the article. She pulled out her laptop and opened it up, scanning the work she'd already done. Some group causing trouble again, objecting to everything the city council was trying to do, and backing the newcomer to the council, Barden, who was upending all they'd been doing. But he had his supporters and they continued to cause trouble. Same old, same old.

She opened her email, looking for a quote from their spokesman. Yes, there was response to her question—not from the actual spokesman but from another man in the group whom she'd contacted. She scanned his answer. It didn't really fit the angle Kevin wanted—and frankly, the one she herself thought was more accurate. *The spokesman did not respond to our request for a comment,* she typed into the story.

Something rustled in the forest.

Danica looked up. The woods had grown dark as she worked. From somewhere back in the trees, she heard a deep breath.

She quickly slammed the lid on her laptop and took it and the wine glass inside. She bolted the lock, wondering if a bear could simply break through the door. She stood, fighting the trembling for a moment, before setting the glass and laptop on the table and crossing to the window to peer out to where she'd heard the sound. She pressed her face to the glass, then suddenly gasped, drawing back.

Was that a face looking back at her? A bear's face? A lynx or bobcat?

Or had she only imagined it? She hurried to the bedroom where another window looked out the same way. Something tall and bear-like lumbered away through the trees—so quietly but for the rustle of leaves as it brushed through them.

Carlton? A bear? It was impossible to know in the dark.

Returning to the front room, she dragged the rocking chair

and end table in front of the glass door. Small protection but at least it was something. She brushed her teeth and crawled under the covers, listening well into the night for any sound outside before finally falling into a deep sleep. One star review for sure. Why hadn't he specified, on his site, that there were *animals* surrounding the place?

The morning brought bright sun and evidence that it had rained. Danica sat up, realizing she must have finally fallen asleep. She rose, feeling groggy without her morning cappuccino, but cautiously pushed aside the curtain.

Nothing moved outside.

She yanked on her skinny jeans and knee-high boots and stuck her head out the front door, looking both ways. Nothing moved.

Bears were nocturnal, he'd said. She stepped out on the deck. The woods were still. She glanced over her left shoulder to the flower gardens far behind Carlton's house. Blooms bobbed and nodded in a light breeze.

Danica crossed the deck, peering carefully over the edge, along the side of the cabin, and into the trees. Nothing moved. Descending the deck stairs, she went around the side of the little house, looking constantly over her shoulder into the trees, ready to bolt. But nothing moved. She studied the earth under the living room window and moved on to the bedroom window. There was no sign of anything.

Maybe, she thought, she'd imagined it all.

She laughed uneasily, muttering, "You're such a city girl."

But she stayed inside to write.

After a long morning working on the article, Danica got up to stretch. She glanced out the window toward Carlton's house and gardens. The day was bright and the flowers swayed as if dancing together. The fears that had kept her in all morning suddenly seemed ridiculous in light of such a beautiful sight.

He'd invited her to go look at the flowers any time. The website had specifically sold the gardens as one of the perks of this place. She slipped her manicured toes into her sandals and headed out of the cabin, up the shell path.

The scent of thousands of blooms reached her long before she got to the garden gate. Once inside, the aroma only grew more scintillating. Danica found herself leaning over now a lily, now a rose, and then over a cluster of black-eyed Susan. They almost seemed to be smiling at her—welcoming her.

Danica shook her head sharply. "What is wrong with me?" she whispered to herself. She'd always been the practical type— not prone to flights of imagination at all. She walked a bit further down the path, till she came to a bench and sat down.

"Was everything comfortable in your cabin?"

Danica jumped, startled, then drew in a sharp breath. Carlton stood beside the bench, in a pair of worn overalls, looking down at her. "You scared me!" Her voice came out sharply. "Actually, there was something in the woods. I didn't sleep well at all."

He shrugged. "It's the woods. I did say there'll be critters out there. They won't hurt you none."

Disdain filled Danica. *Won't hurt you none.* She'd have a good laugh with Kelly and Sue about this bumpkin when she got home.

"The garden will set you right again," he said. "These flowers are like my children. They bring peace to a world that can be ugly. They make things beautiful again."

"Mm-hm."

"Did you want to take a look and learn some of the flowers' names?" he asked.

Irritation grew. She'd wanted to sit here in solitude. Danica shook her head. "I have to get back to work."

Hitting *send* on the city council article, Danica poured herself a glass of white wine. Just 'critters,' she told herself, and, with the sun still bright in the early evening, she took her laptop to the deck to check the responses to last week's article.

This was not what A.B. Conley said, wrote the first commenter. She had quoted Conley in the article. *You took two things he said at separate times and strung them together to make it sound like he said the exact opposite of what he did.*

Very slanted writing, wrote another. *To call someone 'slightly hysterical' is not news reporting. We all saw the video clip and there was nothing hysterical about his demeanor at all. He was calm and factual.*

"Idiots," Danica muttered. A vein throbbed in her temple.

This article left out some very important data from the Journal of the American Medical Association that says exactly the opposite of what the writer is claiming. Did you do any research or just want to push a narrative?

Danica opened her anonymous account and responded to each.

Clearly he said both those things. If you can't understand context and misinterpret and think he didn't say those things, nobody in the comments can help your lack of intelligence.

To the second comment she wrote: *A blind man could see he was hysterical. Did you even watch the same video the rest of the world did? Guess we can't expect any better from you moron Barden-supporters.*

And to the third: *The figures from JAMA have been misconstrued. The articles claiming they said the opposite have been de-bunked. Try to keep up.*

Danica fumed. These fools who supported Barden—nothing but a bunch of small-minded neanderthal haters. She *hated* that man! He did nothing but lie and his idiot troglodyte followers bought it all. Worked up now, she went on YouTube and unleashed on a few more of the neanderthal Bardenistas, but it only fueled her anger.

She looked up at the sky. Before the cabin, it was growing dim. She turned around to see the sun sinking, painting streaks of pink and orange on the western horizon behind the gardens. She took a sip of her wine, glaring at the streaks of brilliant pink and orange across the sky. Those damn Bardenistas even knew how to blow a beautiful sunset. One of them lived next door to her, back at home. She'd taken his damn signs down two or three times now and he kept putting them right back up. He didn't learn.

She glanced at the sky again. It was now a deep, dusky blue in the east. Thinking of last night, she rose from the table and headed back into the cabin. No need to repeat last night's scare.

Deep in research for her next article, Danica bent over her laptop on the kitchen table, sipping her wine now and then.

Suddenly, a chill inched up her spine. She swore she felt a presence at the window on her right side. Goosebumps rose on her arm. She pulled the blinds quickly, spun, and drew the blinds at all the windows in the place. This time, she didn't look outside.

A second bright morning brought a second search under the windows. This time it hadn't rained. Just feet from the window, Danica saw two prints in the dirt. The chill shot sharply up her spine. She spun without looking closely. Was it that oaf Carlton looking in her window? Was the old man a pervert on top of being uneducated? Or was it someone else?

In the cabin, she threw her things in her bag, scooped her toiletries and makeup off the bathroom shelf, and within fifteen minutes had her car packed.

"I want a refund." Danica planted her hands on her hips, glaring up at Carlton. "Twice now, I've felt someone at the window watching me."

"There are...."

"I know, I know, there are *critters* in the woods." She spit out the backwater word. "I don't think it was a chipmunk."

"Being out here can be unnerving when you're used to the

city," he said placidly. "You're sure you don't want to just sit in the garden a spell? I can...."

"There were footprints under my window," she snapped.

Without a word, the big man ambled over toward her cabin. He squatted down, studying the ground. "These?" He looked up, smiling. "Looks like a deer was pretty close."

Danica looked. Hoof prints marked the ground. She frowned, shaking her head in denial. But then—she hadn't looked that closely. She'd panicked and run. She covered her confusion with anger. "I don't know what's going on here, but I want a refund."

Carlton shrugged. "I only refund with twenty-four hour notice. I'll make an exception for you, though and refund the last four nights, though, if you're leaving today."

"A *full* refund," she insisted. "The two nights I've stayed here someone's been looking in my window."

"It was a deer," he said, unruffled. "Just animals in the woods."

"A full refund or you'll be hearing from my lawyer."

Carlton shrugged. "I'm sorry, I don't give refunds because there are animals in the woods." He smiled. "I'll gladly give you a bouquet to take home for your trouble."

"I don't want a damn bouquet," she snapped. "You'll be hearing from my lawyer."

Carlton sighed. "Anger always comes back on the one who is angry."

Danica all but launched herself into the driver's seat of her Volvo and slammed her foot on the gas.

Two weeks passed—no sign of the refund. In between drinks with friends and churning out more articles, Danica checked with her credit card company and several lawyers.

"His policy is clear," the credit card company told her.

"It's not a case you'd win," each of the lawyers told her. "He was generous to refund the nights you didn't stay."

The man who had answered her email two weeks ago about the city council issue was kicking up a fuss—saying she lied in her article when she said they hadn't answered her. It didn't matter. They were stupid Bardenistas. Her boss had her back, firing back at the man, "She said your spokesman didn't respond to a request for comment and that's true."

"He asked me to take care of it because his daughter was in the hospital. We *did* give you a comment and you lied."

"The *spokesman* did *not* give a comment," she barked into the phone. "We did *not lie.* Call our lawyers if you have anything else to say."

"Fools," Danica said with her friends that evening as they sipped cocktails at a bar. With the third, she began to unwind. With the fourth, she began to feel a thrill of pleasure and mirth running through her. The truth was, she was pleased to be able to spite them by saying—quite honestly—that their spokesman had declined to give a comment. She didn't want to give their weak arguments any validity or have some stupid reader actually believing them. "I'm surrounded by morons. You should have heard the stupid coming out of the mouth of the last guy I met off the dating site."

Kelly and Sue rolled their eyes as one.

Danica lifted her hand, catching the waiter's eye and pointing to her empty drink.

Kelly swirled a tiny straw through her cocktail. "The last guy I went out with…. Oh *no,* honey*!*" She waved a hand. "*Oh no.* He seemed like a really great guy—funny, good-looking—so hot!— great job. Smart. We were having this great conversation and you know, so much in common. Then he says he voted Barden."

Danica and Sue groaned.

Over Kelly's head, the TV switched to a new scene. A heavy, bearded man in jeans and a polo shirt stood in front of rows and rows of potted plants on tiered shelves.

Danica sat up straighter in surprise. "That's him!" she exclaimed. The waiter set her fifth drink in front of her.

Sue and Kelly twisted on their stools to look at the TV. "Who?" asked Sue.

"Your last date?" Kelly snorted at her own joke. "He's a little old for you."

"The flower freak." Danica lifted the drink, sipping it down, her eyes glued to the television.

"We're here live in Miami at the International Floriculture Expo," the reporter said, "talking with one of the world's leading experts in the field, Carlton Lester, the former head of Cornell's agriculture department. He's here in Miami all week and we're excited to talk to him."

He nodded, smiling at the camera. "Thanks, Maria."

"What brought you to gardening?" she asked.

Danica, Kelly, and Sue all stared as he answered. The waiter set another drink in front of Danica. She lifted it absently to her lips, staring at the television.

"Bringing beauty into the world," he said. "The world is a hard place with people who can be full of anger and take it out on others."

Danica snorted. "Yeah, like *him*. And he's a perv, too."

"I take empty fields, I take manure—I take the ugly things of life and turn them into something beautiful that gives people joy. I've seen hearts and minds healed in my gardens. They're my pride and joy."

Danica's hand suddenly shot out, gripping Kelly's arm. "They just said he's in Miami all week!"

"Yeah, so?" Kelly asked.

"If he won't give me a refund, I'll take my own! He'll wish he had!"

Sue and Kelly glanced at each other.

"What are you going to do?" Sue asked.

Grinning, Danica tossed back the last of her drink and snatched her car keys out of her purse.

Danica made one stop at her home before heading north. It was a two hour drive—and well worth it, she thought with glee. She suggested once to herself that maybe she should wait until she was completely sober before doing this—make sure she wasn't doing anything *too* stupid. But she had time *now* and he was only at the flower deal for another few days. Besides, they were just flowers.

She almost laughed out loud, thinking of the look on his face when he came home. He deserved it, having cheated her out of her refund. Two lousy, restless nights—it was hardly the place of rest and peace he'd advertised. He should have his license pulled. Her plan would certainly help put this shyster out of business.

She arrived with the moon still high in the sky.

The driveways leading up to the two cabins were both empty. Danica smiled, hitting the gas to speed up to Carlton's. She snatched the large knife from the passenger seat and marched smartly up the shell path. The stars and moon shone down over the gardens. Their light glinted off the white petals of the daisies and etched gold on the sunflowers' edges.

She'd start at the back—patches here and there.

She marched down the path to the back of the garden, grasped the stems of a bunch of black-eyed Susan in her left hand and put the blade to their stalks.

~ ~ ~

Sue and Kelly huddled together in the detective's office. Sue patted at her eyes now and again with a tissue. Danica's editor paced behind them.

"She just didn't show up," Kevin said for the second time. "She's *never* not shown up. She's a hundred percent reliable."

"What happened when you tried to call her?" the detective asked.

"Straight to voicemail every time. No answer. I mean, if she'd answered, would we be here?"

"I think she was going back to that cabin last night," Sue said. "That guy on TV. Lester something."

"Do you know where the cabin is?"

Sue and Kelly shook their heads. "It was some guy, like an air BNB or something and he'd cheated her. She was going to talk to him."

"In the middle of the night?"

Kelly looked down at her knees. "She'd had a little too much to drink. Maybe she just took a nap in a rest area. Can the police look for her car?"

"It was found in a rest area about half an hour north of here," the detective said.

"Well, you have to do *something!*"

"Ma'am." The detective sighed heavily. "We will, we *are*. We're talking to you, right? Getting information."

Sue bolted to her feet. "But we're sitting here *talking!* Why aren't you out there looking for her!" She crumpled back into her chair, crying.

~ ~ ~

Carlton pulled on his overalls and strode out to his garden, glad to be home. He'd long ago lost his taste for these conventions and shows and forums. He just wanted to be in his peaceful little bit of Eden. He strode out to his garden, easing the gate open and beaming with joy at his Hyacinths, his Daisies and black-eyed Susans, and Ivies on overhead trellises; Roses of every variety and some he'd created himself, Lilies and sprinklings of Edelweiss and a rainbow of tulips and foxgloves and gardenia and Holly.

He beamed at them all, walking slowly down the path. "Every one of you perfect, beautiful," he said happily. He glanced up at the blue skies. "Did you eat well while I was away? Was there a bit of rain?" He stooped heavily to look at Hyacinth, touching its leaves. "Ah, you're looking so much happier than last time I saw you! I think I see you smiling now!"

He continued his walk down the shell path. The noon sun shone brightly on his beautiful flowers as he squatted by one or another, admiring them and talking to them.

He came at last to the end of the acre of blooms and dropped to one knee before a Rose of Sharon of near-white petals fading out to a dark pink at their edges. "Ah, what is this! A new flower in my garden! Where did you come from?"

He frowned down at it. "Hibiscus syriacus Danicaz. Where *did* you come from?" His eyes fell on the kitchen knife lying amongst the hyacinths.

He stared at it a moment before lifting his eyes back to the Danicaz. "I did try to tell you." He shook his head sadly. "I hope you'll be happy here. There's a peace and tranquility....something you won't find in the cities."

The Knight and the Wolf

In life, we sometimes fail. Some of us only a little bit and some of us much more. I like to believe that every person strives to do better.
This story is dedicated to Richard John.

Conchobar was well-named. *Hound* and *desiring*. These things summed up his life.

He was my kin—and a sadder boy you'd be hard-pressed to find although of course, those were hard days. How many fathers were loving to their sons? Many were, in the hard way of warriors. But many weren't. Conchobar's father was the town regent and a harder heart you've never seen.

It was a hot July, the one that Conchabar turned twelve—three years after he'd come to live with my family, taking care of the stables at my father's inn —that the night was broken by the shouts of men and a horrible stench in the air.

I went to my window to see Conchabar standing in the cobbled street, staring down it to his father's home. Under the full moon, I could see it had burned. Guilt shot through me. I had done nothing to stop it.

A great gray animal, as big and shaggy as a wolf, padded up the street. Conchabar stared at it, unafraid. It came to him, so big its head reached to just below his chin. They stared at each other. The boy put his hand deep into the fur of the big animal and they stood a moment, nose to nose, before the wolf lay down at his feet with a whimper.

Conchabar stared down the street at the burned shell of the place that had once been his home, at the men shouting and yelling around it. He turned and went into the stables, the wolf following him. He didn't wait to see, as I did, that the men carried his father's body out of the house.

From that day on, the big dog was always at his side.

They stood silently, he and the dog, watching, the next day, as the priest sprinkled holy water on his father's coffin and as it was lowered into the ground behind the church. Conchabar turned to the animal and said, "I will call you *Fuascailt.*"

When village boys taunted Conchabar in the market the following week, Fuascailt growled, baring its teeth. Conchabar was never again taunted.

In August, I brought food to the men working in the stables. Conchabar cleaned stalls while two of the older men worked with a new horse. As I set the food down on a table by the door, Fuascailt suddenly woofed at Conchabar.

"Hush, Fuascailt," the boy said.

The dog would not hush. It rushed at him, taking his sleeve between his teeth, pulling.

Moments later, the angry horse bucked, flinging off both its handlers, and kicked into the air right where Conchabar had stood.

The men, scrambling up off the floor, stared at the dog. "He knew," one of them whispered.

Fuascailt turned on the horse, letting out a low growl. The beast suddenly settled. It let out one last defiant *neigh* and then seemed to pull back into itself. Conchabar approached fearlessly. The horse tossed its head but at the low rumble rising from Fuascailt's throat, it dropped its nose meekly to its chest.

"There now, you'll be happier to let us give you dinner and a nice bed," Conchabar said, and led it into its stall and closed the door.

The men looked at Conchabar with something between awe and fear.

Within weeks, the boy and his wolf-dog were in demand with horse owners wanting him to work with their most spirited animals.

Through it all, I held a guilt and fear deep inside. I wondered if I was mad. And I thought of Athelyna's words, that July day I saw her come out from the forest, from a path that led to only one place—and a place no good Christian would go. *Is it evil to stop evil?* She had asked me, one slender black eyebrow arched, and a slight smile on her lips.

Her father—Conchabar's father—was an evil man. He drank far too much, as had his father before him.

He terrorized his wife, a wee mouse of a woman, berating her, beating her, throwing the meals she cooked for him on the floor.

He terrorized his four daughters. As they and I sat at our sewing one day, he went into a rage over some imagined slight or failure and threw Edan across the room. She landed dangerously near the fire, and in scrambling away from it, tripped, such that the edge of her skirt caught the flame. It glowed there in the blue dyed cloth, the glow spreading as we all watched, too stunned to move.

Suddenly, Conchobar, no more than nine years of age, leapt into action, throwing himself at his sister, rolling her away from the fire, and snatching his father's ale off the table to douse her dress before it could burst into flame.

Donchabar backhanded him with a mighty roar. "My ale, boy! You wasted my ale!"

Conchobar, looking up at his father from the floor, said mildly, "Would you ha' had your daughter burn alive, Father?"

Donchabar flung the pewter mug at his son. It struck him in the temple. "Get out," he said. "Never come back."

Conchobar rose gravely from the floor, giving his father a bow. "Yes, Father," was all he said.

I sat glued to my stool, the sewing shaking in my hands. Only when Donchabar turned his back did I cast a swift glance at my kinswomen, all five of them pale and silent, and race from the house myself, lifting my skirts to hurry through the narrow streets of the town.

I found Conchobar where I thought he'd be. He sat in the stables behind my father's inn, eating an apple with one hand, and the other buried in the thick curling fur of a hound that lay at his side. Donchabar had killed a dog several years before when it attacked him as he struck his wife. He would not allow dogs near his property. He hated dogs more than anything—except perhaps his wife and children.

"My father will take you in," I said.

"Aye, I imagine he will." Conchobar spoke as if nothing of any moment had happened.

That was how he had come to live with us, these past years.

It was several months after the fire, just before the snow fell, that my father received a visit from Earl Theobald himself.

He settled into a booth not far from the fire, set back where prying eyes could not peer too easily at our esteemed visitor. My father opened his best mead. My mother hastened to prepare our finest venison and rabbit stew, full of the leeks and other wonderful vegetables for which her garden was particularly renowned. I could see my father was nervous. One did not always want to attract the attention of the noble class.

I thought of Athelyna coming out of the forest and hoped she had not, somehow, been found out. Perhaps I was not the only one who had seen her come from that path. The earl was known to be a devout man. He would not like to know of such goings-on in any of his lands.

I peered from behind the bar, catching their words.

They spoke, as they ate, of the weather, crops, news of highwaymen recently preying on travelers and what the earl planned on doing about it. They spoke of the threats of King Edward across the sea.

Finally, the earl finished his last bite and sighed. "The best meal I've had in a long time!" He smiled, wiping his great beard with a big cloth. "I hear you've a boy of great skill with horses," he said.

My father stared for a moment. I could see that he wondered if this was good news or bad news, that our Conchabar had come to the earl's attention.

He nodded slowly. "He does indeed seem to have a gift. He and the dog."

The earl arched an eyebrow. "The dog?"

"They are a pair," my father said. "They work together."

"I should like to meet this remarkable pair."

"Bellaflor!" My father raised his voice. I shrank into the shadows as my mother hurried from the kitchens. "Get the boy."

My mother glanced with some awe at the earl, giving him a deep bob of her head, and hurried away, calling for the boy.

The two men drank in silence as they waited. The earl looked pleased. As I studied his face, I believed I saw kindness in his eyes, bright blue with wrinkles just beginning at the corners. He was a fierce warrior, they said. But I saw a man who seemed at peace with himself and life. I felt good about whatever he wanted with Conchabar and I thought back to that day he had joined our family.

I imagined, as I saw him eating that apple in my father's stables, three years hence, that despite his calm words, I could feel the heaviness in his heart as it closed a portion of itself to the world.

He had risen with a sigh, that day. "It's not me I mind," he said, "but that there's now no one to protect my sisters." He followed me into the house and from that day onward, my father treated him as his own beloved son, though Conchobar worked hard, never feeling he had the same full right to be there, as did my seven brothers, my sister, and myself.

He was always peaceful. He often smiled. He slipped apples to the poor children of the town or gave them work helping with the horses or pleaded with my mother to give the girls odd jobs to earn money for their families.

Yet as we grew, I sensed the deepest sorrow within him—a profound desire for what the human soul says we should all have —parents who love us.

His mother died the next year in childbirth. His sisters grew in their own way. Bencelina seemed to withdraw, to float somehow in a world of her own, retreating to the shadows when her father went into his rages. She was beautiful and within years married a young man of the town, a merchant's son, who treated her with the love a wife deserves.

Edan, being quick and bright, found employ in the Earl's home, sewing with the women there.

Honora took up her novitiate, the moment she was able, in the abbey.

It was Athelyna, with her raven hair and piercing dark eyes— the one Donchabar seemed to leave alone—who stayed.

"My Lord."
All eyes lifted to the boy who stood in the doorway of the

kitchens, with the big gray animal at his side.

The earl drew in a breath. "Mary, Joseph, and all the saints! Is that a dog or a wolf?" he asked.

My father studied the animal for a moment before saying, "In truth, my lord, I suppose we know not. However, it's never shown any aggression to any but those who intend harm."

"Come here, Boy." The earl beckoned.

Conchabar came forward in his usual calm way. Fuascailt walked beside him as if they were one. When Conchabar offered a deep bow to the earl, the dog also dropped its head low. The earl stared at it, a smile playing across his lips. "You've taught your beast court manners, then?"

"My Lord," said the boy, "I've taught him nothing."

"What do you call him?"

"Fuascailt."

Theobald frowned. "Redemption? Why do you call a beast like this *Redemption*?"

"I know not, my Lord," Conchabar said. He lifted his hand to drop it in the great gray ruff around the wolf's neck. "I only know that when he looked at me, the word came into my mind and it seemed that that was what he wanted to be called."

"Are you fanciful, Boy?" the earl asked.

"I do not believe I am, Sir," Conchabar replied. "Perhaps I was that night, but as a rule, I would say I am not. I cannot say, in the matter of Fuascailt's name whether I was or not."

Theobald smiled. "Then we shall believe that perhaps you were led. Redemption is a fine thing. As one who is charged with fighting battles and making many difficult decisions that affect others, I strive each day for redemption from any mistakes I have made or any harm I have brought on others. Redemption is something we must all seek, every day."

"Yes, my Lord," Conchabar said.

The earl stared at him a moment, his head tilted, as if he wanted to say something else on the matter. Then he cleared his throat and I believed he had changed his mind. "You and this beast of yours—I'm told you handle horses better than men three times your age."

Conchabar bowed his head. "It is Fuascailt, really."

"The boy does not give himself credit," my father said. The fire flickered over his face and I saw pride glowing there. I thought how sad that in these three years, Conchabar could never believe he was as loved as my father's own sons. How sad that that hole was always in his heart and soul.

"The stallion nearly kicked his head off," my father boasted, "and yet the moment the wolf growled at the horse, the moment it settled, our Conchabar walked up to it as if naught had happened."

"Mmm." Theobald stroked his beard, studying Conchabar, who stood silent, watching the earl in return. "I like you more and more, Boy," the earl said. "I had come here to bring you back to work with my horses. They are war horses. They are, by nature, strong, strong-willed, and aggressive. Yet they must also be trained. But I think there's more to you than that."

My father leaned forward in his chair.

Theobald's eyes narrowed as if in thought, as if he chose his words carefully. "Despite your youth, I see before me not a boy, but a man—a man of honor, courage, and humility. I see a peace about you. I propose that you work with my horses, yes, but I also offer you the opportunity to become a page and start the path toward knighthood."

Conchabar drew in a deep breath even as he fell to one knee. Fuascailt dropped to the floor beside him. "My Lord, I am not of noble blood."

"Rise," Theobald commanded. When Conchabar did, the wolf likewise rising to his feet, the earl said, "I am of the mind that there is not only noble blood, but noble character. I prefer the latter. I see great potential in you. These are trying times and I would be a fool not to have a man like you at my side."

"Fuascailt can come with me?" the boy asked.

"I understand you work together. Aye. He comes with you. I would have it no other way."

Conchabar fell to his knee again, taking the earl's hands between his. "Thank you, my lord! Thank you! You do me great honor and I will do my best to always serve you faithfully and well."

Fuascailt woofed and I swore for a moment the animal smiled. It turned its big shaggy head and its eyes bored right into mine. Did it even wink? My heart trembled. *Are you fanciful*, the earl had asked. Yes—yes, I was fanciful. It was only my fear speaking, because such a thing could not happen! Yet I felt joy and pride coming from that dog. Wolf. Whatever it was.

The earl turned then, also looking right at me. He smiled. "I expect you can bring us a round of mead, Lass, to celebrate?"

I hastened away, embarrassed at having been caught.

In the following years, Conchabar came home to visit only now and again. The earl's castle was not so far away. But his work and his training were rigorous, starting several years behind the other pages as he did.

The years passed quickly. I married Mochan, the baker's son —and I fought my conscience as I knelt to give my confession the night before the marriage.

Conchabar's father died in a fire. Could I have stopped it? I fled that night in fear of what I had seen. I never told anyone what Athelyna had done. Was I as guilty, hiding her dealings with the old woman in the forest?

Only good seemed to have come to Conchabar since that night. Yet—what was Athelyna really dealing in? Could good come from evil? They said the woman in the forest was evil. Satan, Father told us, could come disguised as an angel of light.

We attended Conchabar's knighting ceremony, though as mere innkeepers and bakers, we stayed well at the back of the great hall. Bencelina and her merchant husband had grown wealthy and stood closer to the front. Edan, as one of the women in waiting, was also closer to the front, as was Honora, a respected nun now serving as the trusted aide to the elderly abbess and gaining her own renown for her holiness.

Athelyna—well, I spotted her farther back even than we. She had neither married nor gone to the convent. She lived, peculiarly alone in her father's house that had been rebuilt from the fire. I never knew how she survived. Sometimes I saw young girls step furtively to her door and slip in, looking around as they did. Sometimes it was older women with sorrow in their eyes. Now and again, a young man entered her home.

She attended Mass daily, her head bowed in deep prayer. Few people spoke to her.

I often thought of that night. She had never seen me enter or leave as she spoke with her father. Did she ever wonder why I shied away from her? Did she know, somehow, that I had seen and heard?

Did she notice the way others avoided her? If she did, she seemed not to care.

She grew, if possible, only more radiant with the years, a light of peace seeming to shine from her very countenance.

England invaded and Conchabar, nine years after that fateful day, went into battle against men twice his age. The stories came to our small village. They spread to England: The boy who fought with a wolf at his side. The wolf who leapt and pulled the Knight's enemies from their horses. The Wolf who savaged any who threatened Sir Conchabar. The Wolf who dragged his knight from certain death, time and again.

The stories came to our small village: How older and greater knights took heart when they saw the Knight and the Wolf take their places in their ranks. How armies cheered when they saw Conchabar and Fuascailt arrive.

He was the Cú Chulainn of our age.

Bit by bit, our small armies pushed back the invaders.

I began to have hope that my three small children might grow up in a land of peace, unlike I had.

The Knight and his Wolf became legend, giving our people hope and striking fear into the hearts of the enemy. Sometimes travelers came to our inn telling us of their travels. But soon, they asked us about Conchubar and it became apparent their real pilgrimage was to the home of the Knight and his Wolf. Our prestige grew. Our business grew.

The years passed and my father lay dying. My brothers gathered around. I sat, heavily pregnant with my fourth child, and Mochan at my side, holding one hand as my other clutched my father's. I looked up to the sound at the door and there stood Conchabar and Fuascailt at his side. The beast whose nose had once reached a boy's chin now reached to just above his elbow. He was strong, with muscles bulging in his arms. His hair, auburn and wavy, fell below his shoulders. He had a red beard, growing full even in his youth.

I stared at the dog. It had changed, I thought. I remembered the first night I saw it—how he laid down at Conchabar's feet. Why, I wondered, with my father's hand warm in mine, did I suddenly think that the dog of that night was fearful and meek in a way it no longer was? This was an animal that now stood proud and strong beside its master. The boy, too, once meek and mild had become strong and confident.

He had strength, Conchabar did—but he still had humility and peace. He dropped to his knee at my father's side. He first touched my cheek, saying, "I'm so sorry; he was such a good man," and then turned to take my father's other hand. He kissed the withered old cheek and whispered, "Thank you."

My father's eyes fluttered open. "I wish you could have known how much I wanted to be a father to you," he whispered.

My mother leaned forward with a towel soaked in cold ale

and touched it to his lips.

"You suffered, thinking your father didn't love you. And maybe he didn't."

Fuascailt whimpered and settled his haunches uneasily onto the floor beside Conchabar. He licked Conchabar's arm.

My father cleared his throat weakly. "But I loved you as I loved my own sons and I wished you could have seen that you were loved as much as any of them."

Conchabar bowed his head over my father's hand. I saw his shoulders quiver. "Sometimes we can only see things with age," he whispered.

The dog laid its big head against his arm.

"Why did my father hate me so?" he asked.

The dog whimpered, and pawed at him.

My father pulled his hand from mine to grasp Conchabar's. He half-raised himself, his eyes piercing the Knight's. "He didna hate you, my son. He hated his own weakness. I knew him as a boy. His father was worse than he was. He beat him and drank. Your father became what he hated and he hated himself for it." My father sank back.

The dog whimpered and nuzzled its nose under Conchabar's elbow.

"Stop," the Knight whispered to the dog. Fuascailt whined and lay down, lifting his deep brown eyes to the knight and the dying man.

My father's eyes met mine. "The world is not what you think," he whispered. He drew a breath and his chest became still. My heart ached. I wanted to scream, to cry, to plead with God, "No! I need my father! Just another week, but another day! I need him!"

I looked at Conchabar, bowed over my father's corpse. I wished he'd had what I had. I wished he'd seen that he *did* have what I had—a father who loved him.

Athelyna came into the room. She looked at the Wolf. It met her eyes, then dropped to the floor, watching her.

"I'm sorry," Athelyna whispered. "He was a good man."

Her eyes met mine, and I felt that long-ago secret between us.

* * *

It was the summer of our fifteenth summer, three years after Conchobar came to live with my family, that I saw her coming out of the woods behind the town. I stared. There was only one thing down that path from which she came, and the whole village knew it to be evil. The old woman who brewed potions lived far back along that trail.

Athelyna's eyes met mine boldly. Her lips curved into a small smile.

She was a great beauty—yet there was something about her that kept the young men at a distance. I never knew for sure if she wanted it that way and held them off herself or if they sensed something in her that made them fearful. She was a strong presence—that was true. There was a boldness to her that left one unsure.

"What do you fear I've been doing?" she asked, taking a step nearer me.

My breath dragged into my body with a shudder. Chills went down my arms. Her father, I thought.

Athelyna nodded slowly. "I think you know."

"Surely ye canna tarry with the evil they say she does," I said.

"Is it evil to stop evil?" Athelyna asked. One slender black eyebrow arched.

I found a reason, that evening, to pass by their house. I feared her intentions. As I stood in the hall, having let myself in as I had over the years, I heard her voice and his. "Ungrateful bastard," he roared.

"Father, *you* kicked him out when he was but a child and told him never to return. He did exactly as you yourself told him to."

"A boy should know when words are spoken in anger at his own defiance and know to come home and ask forgiveness."

"For saving his sister's life?" Athelyna sounded amused.

Donchabar mumbled something. I peered around the corner just on time to see him slam his tankard down on the table. Athelyna took it up, gliding to a keg in the corner to re-fill it. I saw her tip some powder in from a cloth sachet she held in her hand. Fear grew in me, wondering if I should stop this. Whatever it was came from the woman in the woods.

Surely she meant to kill him.

She set the ale back before him, watching as he snatched it up and drank deeply.

I waited. She waited. Donchabar shuddered suddenly.

At this, Athelyna spoke. "Surely, Father, you are not as hard-hearted as all that? Surely you have some love in your heart for your only son?"

The big man stiffened. He drew a ragged breath and suddenly gulped another great draft of his ale. His lips stiffened.

"Remember the pride you had the day he was born?" the girl asked. "I remember, Father, how you ran through the streets shouting that you had a son after four daughters."

"He should have come home like a dutiful son to help with the work," Donchabar said gruffly.

"Will you not speak to him and tell him you're sorry?" Athelyna spoke the words almost as if in a chant. A spell, I thought. She was weaving some spell over him.

Suddenly, he burst into tears, his shaggy gray head falling to the table, and sobs racking his body.

Athelyna stood, a space between them, watching. "You miss him," she chanted softly. "Tell him you're sorry. Ask him to come home."

Suddenly Donchabar shot to his feet. His face was near purple with rage at the same time tears streamed down his cheeks. "I will *not,"* he said. He glanced at the tankard and thrust it at her. "Get me more."

"It is the ale that has been your undoing," she said. "It has cost you your whole family."

"You're still here."

"You have far too much pride to admit to him that you were wrong." Athelyna took the tankard to the corner and re-filled it. She looked up at her father. "I will give you the freedom to go beyond your pride, if you canna do it yourself."

"He's stayed away too long," Donchabar retorted. "He's not welcome here."

"Do you want my help?" she asked.

"I will not ask him back!" he shouted.

But tears streamed down his face.

Athelyna tipped another bit of powder into his ale as he watched. "Do you want my help?" she asked softly, handing it back to him.

He stared at her a long moment. Then he took the chalice. His eyes on hers, he gulped it down.

In the shadows of the hall, I turned and fled, as silently as I could. I had failed to stop her. I was part of whatever evil she had concocted.

* * *

Conchabar clutched my father's hands in his and dropped his head on my father's still chest. "Thank you," he said. "Thank you for being a father to me."

In front of me, Fuascailt rose. He lifted his nose to the sky and let out a long, mournful howl.

Athelyna dropped to her knees before the big animal. They gazed at each other a long moment, before she buried her arms in its ruff. "Well done," she said. "Well done, Fuascailt."

The Sparrow

The diver shook his head. "Naming her after Captain Jack's ship was the *first* mistake." He chomped on a cigar more appropriate to one at least twice his age. The sun reached through dirty windows to glint off his copper hair. "Bad omen from the start."

Mark glanced at his wife. Nothing about this diving operation was what they'd expected, starting with the place, one they'd never heard of despite years diving to shipwrecks, turning up unexpectedly on their GPS. They certainly hadn't expected anyone so young to be running the operation.

"Pirates of the Caribbean didn't come out until 2003," Melinda said. "The Sparrow disappeared well before that."

"Sure did." The boy stubbed his cigar out with a vicious stab and rose. "Her builder knew the scriptwriter. *Idiot!*" He pulled his suit up as he headed for the door.

Tom cinched his diving belt tighter. "It's like it's personal," he muttered to Melinda as they followed.

They crossed the small highway, fins flapping against their thighs, out to a rickety dock stretching into Lake Superior to board a motor boat. As it sputtered and started across gray waves, Tom gazed over the water. *The Sparrow*—the elusive jewel in their wreck-hunting crown! "Bold claim," he said as the kid steered the craft. Extensive searches had turned up no sign of the wreck in all these years. "If you know where it is, why don't you tell the authorities?"

"I like my exclusive right to take treasure hunters." The boy grinned over his shoulder. "Plus—I'm exclusive about who I take. Gotta trust 'em." His smile disappeared. "Trust matters."

"You must have been a baby when it went down," Mark said.

"How do you know about *The Sparrow*?" the kid asked.

"Stories from divers." One diver in particular, Mark thought: His father. He'd sought Captain Amos Jameson's lost ship with a passion that bordered on manic, confiding to Mark before his last dive—the one from which he never returned—what the ship's real cargo had been.

The kid stared straight ahead. "What do you know about her?"

"Same as everyone. Disappeared, no mayday, no crew ever washed up."

"They were betrayed."

"Betrayed?" Melinda's voice rose in surprise. "How?"

"Her captain agreed to carry a load for a friend. Share the profit." He gazed out over the rippling water for long moments before continuing, "The friend sent pirates to take the whole cargo, instead."

Melinda glanced at Mark.

"Huh!" he said. A chill pinched his spine.

The sun was high when their guide eased back on the throttle. "Ready?" He looked back over his shoulder as he dropped the anchor.

"Never readier!" Melinda's face shone with excitement.

Mark beamed, pleased to be able to share this dream with her. His own heart beat faster in expectation.

The pictures alone, of the lost ship, would net them a fortune. The guide had forbidden cameras. But a life in underwater research had its benefits.

Melinda had her fins on. She snapped the webbed straps of the air tanks. She grinned and popped the regulator into her mouth. The three of them flipped backward off the boat and entered the silent world below the waves.

Husband and wife glanced at one another, gave a thumbs up, and kicked strong legs, following their guide to where the water grew murky. They switched on their headlamps.

And there it was below: a great tanker, settled among walleye and pike floating languidly past. Mark swam to the helm, rubbing with gloved hand. SPAR appeared in gold letters. He wiped more and found ROW. Melinda met his eyes, a smile showing around her regulator, and touched her belt. First picture!

They twisted in the water and flipped after the boy, who glided over the top of the tanker. Melinda snapped picture after picture, stopping often.

Wonder filled Mark. Apart from their guide, no one had seen the *Sparrow* in over two decades. She had carried gold, not the ore claimed. Mark wondered if the boy had found the hold. He drew a beacon from his belt and attached it firmly to the ship's side while Melinda floated ahead, distracting the guide.

Mark's heart raced as they reached a great maw where a grate should have been. They jackknifed and dove into the ship's interior. Mark nodded at Melinda and she swam away from the men. The guide pointed; Mark nodded and followed. They passed the galley and sleeping quarters, where men floated, preserved by the cold water of Superior's ice water mansions. Limbs swayed in the current. They stared glassy-eyed into eternity.

Mark touched his belt repeatedly, snapping pictures. He would get better ones when he and Melinda returned on their own.

He turned, thinking they'd been down a long time, and realized he was alone in the engine room. He gave several strong kicks, searching, but the kid was gone. Mark glanced at his air gauge, surprised to see it had gotten low. And suddenly, the excitement of the past hour turned to a flutter of fear.

Mark swam through the silent tanker, past floating, staring men. The boy had disappeared.

Far down a hall, Melinda's headlamp appeared, giving Mark his first breath of relief. She swam toward him, a question in her eyes. Mark pointed to his air gauge and upward. They kicked through the hall to the main hold at which they'd entered.

A grate now covered the opening.

They glanced at each other and swam toward it. It was tight in place. The flutter of fear turned to the calm that overtook Mark in danger. He shook the grate, pushed; together, they kicked. It wouldn't give.

Beckoning, he led Melinda back through murky halls and holds. They would break the glass in the command tower.

The kid—what was his name? Mark suddenly wondered if they'd ever been told.

They swam up into the command tower. Mark saw immediately that the windows were too small to escape through. Suddenly, Melinda's eyes flew wide. She grabbed his arm, pointing.

Mark stared. His father sat in one chair, wearing a diving suit, horror on his face, appearing to stare at something. Mark's blood froze. He kicked his fins, slowly turning.

In the captain's chair sat their guide, staring endlessly into the sea. He wore a white uniform with gold captain's bars on the shoulder. His auburn hair lifted straight up, swaying in the current. He seemed to smile. The name on his uniform read *Jameson.*

The door of the command room floated languidly shut, sealing them in.

Something in the Woods

This story was inspired by my new home and land. It is, as in the story, full of fantastical creatures, mermaids and crouching pumas, a grove of flamingos and more. It is windows everywhere. One night as I sat writing by the windows, I did hear a strange, guttural sound outside. It inspired this story.

I dedicate this story to Bryan and Betty Flaherty, who, like Emile and Marceau, envisioned and created this wonderful property full of whimsy and fantasy.

Sheila sat in her armchair, looking out the huge picture window—one of many that formed two walls of the great hall in her new house. Beyond the wall of windows lay a wide lawn, a pond with a fountain spraying high in the air, and further still, a wide valley full of trees turning gold, orange, red, and yellow.

Sheila smiled, happy with the surprising turn in her life. She had moved here three months ago in the heat of summer, thrilled at the solitude, the quiet, the beauty—forty acres of land left in her aunt's will, that gave her the peace to write and edit.

Despite the solitude, the town, with all the groceries and supplies she needed, was only a ten minute drive. She had taken to twice a week trips to town—having a coffee, reading the small town's newspaper, and picking up some groceries or light bulbs or whatever she might need.

The small town newspaper intrigued her. It seemed to be a collection of world news mixed with local 4-H events and recipes and what she laughingly thought of as local Bat Boy stories. The stories spoke of *Something* in the woods. Something large. Aggressive. Stories for a paper that had no crime to report. Not that she was complaining about a lack of crime! It was a thrill not to worry if she'd accidentally left a door unlocked.

At the coffee shop, she laid down the latest paper and returned to her laptop, sipping her coffee as she corrected an author's typos and grammar.

"A wolf, my friend Deb said."

The words caught Sheila's ear. She continued scanning the document, with only a quick glance up to see the speaker—a heavy-set woman in a green shirt at least a decade out of style, leaning forward in excitement toward a woman with white hair clipped up. "She says it was dark and bigger than any wolf she's ever seen, but that's what she thought it was."

"Did it go after her?" the older lady asked breathlessly. "I've heard it's been seen quite a few times now. Especially just south of the mountain."

Sheila kept her eyes glued to her monitor, tapping her keys in random order so as to appear not to be listening. Her land was just south of the mountain.

"She was inside," the woman in outdated green said. "But she could hear it snarling out there. She shut the doors right away and hoped the dog didn't have to go out again!"

"To be fair," said the older woman, "Deb's eyesight isn't the best. How sure is she of what she saw?"

"Well!" the woman in green huffed. "The Sentinel wrote the story, didn't they?"

"They did," the older woman agreed. "I'm sure they asked more people. I'm sure they verified it."

"Well, Deb thinks it's unlike anything natural. She heard it snarling out there and one of her chickens was missing the next day."

"I did hear that Ellen May's cat disappeared and her goat was mangled by something in the night. It was all dead, and its body clawed and ripped up in the morning when they found it."

"You know what they say." The older woman's voice dropped. Sheila strained to hear what they said.

"About when it started?" the woman in green whispered.

"Since Emile died!" The older woman hissed the words in a stage whisper easily heard all over the coffee shop. "It's started since she died."

Sheila realized she'd stopped pretending to type, though her eyes were still glued to the screen as she listened. The women glanced at her. Sheila gave them a smile and tapped on more keys.

On returning home, Sheila worked on the garden for an hour, with Pelly, her Newfoundland, romping in the yard or planting herself in the garden beside her. She was grateful she'd let Emile's rabbits and chickens go. She had no desire to care for more animals, especially on the far edge of the property. Why her aunt had kept so many was anyone's guess—as was her strange request in the will regarding them. Sheila felt no guilt for ignoring that.

Wiping her hands on her pants, she returned to the house and after a quick shower, settled in for an evening of working on her own writing. The sun fell away behind her as she worked, her mind jumping between her editing job and the women in the coffee shop.

Pelly nosed at the door, whining. It pulled Sheila from her thoughts of this creature the town said lived in the woods. It was as believable as Big Foot. She rose to push the door open, watching as the Newfie crossed the deck in the evening dusk, descending to the yard and searching around to do her business. Her black coat blended into the dimming light and she disappeared, though she was only a few yards away. Not even her gray patch showed.

Sheila watched, listening as the wind whispered through the trees, rustling the golds and yellows. The forest had become sparser, with the falling of the leaves, so that she could see further into the forest that surrounded her home. Pelly soon came back, pushing her way quickly into the door.

Sheila returned to her armchair and her laptop, turning her mind back to her editing of a horror story about a Sasquatch-type creature in the woods—but something far less benign and reclusive than Sasquatch. Something that hunted people, sought revenge for wrongs done. The author wrote with vivid descriptions that brought the words to life like a movie on the pages. Sheila thought of the Sentinel's series on this creature people had supposedly seen in the woods. It fed her imagination, helping her to add key details to the author's work.

Pelly settled into her dog bed, while cool night air wafted in through the open doors. From outside came sounds of clattering— and a sound as of snarling. Sheila's head shot up, looking into the black reflection of the floor to very high ceiling windows. She'd always been jumpy and prone to flights of imagination. It was likely what made her a good editor and writer.

* * *

It was writing that brought Sheila to this solitary location. Her suburban home had been too full of distractions that cost her both time and money. Too many people, too many events, too much noise. Stories of writers going to the wilderness, retreating from the world, had captured her imagination. Places where you could see the stars! Where a different world surrounded you and your imagination could run free! Where there were fewer distractions!

It was beyond her means, of course.

Then Emile died in a car accident, only 56 years old and long since widowed, leaving her entire estate to Sheila. Sheila didn't have to think twice about moving into the inherited house, rather than selling it.

The proceeds from her own home sale and the sale of all her own things that she would no longer need and had no attachment to, would allow her to live comfortably for several years while working on her writing.

Aunt Emile's house was a fairy tale. The separate garage featured a workroom. The great hall was like something out of a medieval fantasy with a two-story stone fireplace, while the doors were all Frank Lloyd Wright. Outside, a little stream trickled over a waterfall, overlooked by a pair of ceramic mermaids and laughing frogs in overalls with fishing polls. The stream burbled along into a pond with a huge fountain shooting at least six feet up. The wooded trails were full of fanciful creatures—octopi in trees, fairies, monkeys hanging from branches, a wooded cove full of flamingo, life-size pumas and panthers sunning on rocks and a near-life-size Big Foot slouching behind a tree.

Aunt Emile had been largely regarded as the family eccentric. The terms of her will bore that out. The lawyer, a young partner in the firm, had looked at Sheila with his head cocked, before pointing to a line in the document. "It's a key condition of her will that you maintain the rabbits and chickens in the pen at the edge of the woods and open the gate every Saturday night—*all night.*"

"I don't understand," Sheila had said. "If I open the gate, won't they all just head out into the woods? I mean—I've never dealt with chickens and rabbits. But why would I do that?"

The young lawyer shrugged. "It's not ours to understand. We are only here to carry out her terms. Do you agree to do that or do we pass the property on to the secondary inheritor?"

"Sure," Sheila said. She couldn't see the reason, but she was hardly going to lose the chance of a lifetime over such a silly condition.

It was an amazing place—the perfect place. Aunt Emile had left a veritable jungle of plants in the huge sunny great hall and outside on the large deck surrounding the place. She'd left her husband's clothes in his closet and a workshop of her inventions; a photography studio, with frames and matte-cutting equipment; thirty-two musical instruments, including two grand pianos, three harps in various sizes, flutes, saxophones, guitars, and tin whistles; a collection of her compositions; and a large library of at least four thousand books in shelves running the length of a long, narrow hall. An entire section featured French history and French legends.

Sheila had started her days, for the three months since settling in, reading half an hour a morning from this collection that told a part of her heritage her parents had never spoken of. She had immersed herself in Louis and Antoinette, in court intrigue and warfare, as well as mythical creatures she'd never heard of—the shaggy Peluda with its snake's head and serpent tail and porcupine quills, the *feu follet,* the evil *Cheval Mallet* who, as a saddled and bridled horse lured poor travelers to terrible fates, and the *Beast of Gévaudan,* the huge shaggy man-eating wolf whose reign of terror was ended only by Louis XV's hunters. The Le Loup Garou was a man turned into a wolf for failing in his religious duties. Only when someone recognized him in his wolf form and drew blood could he be saved from this punishment—and only then if neither of them ever spoke of it again.

The book containing these stories sat even now on the cushions of the window seat at Sheila's right hand.

Another crash sounded outside, distant and somewhere beyond the deck. Sheila jumped up and shut and locked the door. Only then did she press her hands to the window, peering out into the dark. Her own face stared back at her, oddly framed and mingling with the image of the deck chairs. They all stood upright, exactly where they belonged. So what had fallen?

Sheila grabbed the remote and turned off the interior lights, then hurried to the kitchen for a flashlight. Going up the narrow back stairs to an upper bedroom, she opened a window to sweep the light, a strong, narrow beam, over the deck below and out across the lawn. The wrought iron table and chairs were in place by the pond. There was nothing to explain the crash. The wind was still.

She slid the beam along the forest, flashing in and out of trees. Nothing moved.

Slowly, Sheila tread back down the narrow stairs to the large room below. In the office, she once again flashed the beam out, trying to see if anything was in the woods. Stories from the Sentinel filled her mind. But there was nothing.

She moved back into the great hall. It could have been a wolf, she decided. Maybe a coyote. They were harmless enough. At least if your dog was big enough, which Pelly was. She glanced at the Newfie. The dog lay on her bed, her big brown eyes lifted to Sheila's, unconcerned. Soothed by the dog's calm, Sheila settled back to her work. If something was out there, Pelly would see it.

"I'm glad you could come, Mom," Sheila said. She set two glasses of wine at the cherry and granite table under kitchen lights —each bulb held by a metal man in various positions, standing straddled on a parallel pair of wires.

"Well worth the drive!" Evette beamed. She looked young for her 55 years. "It's quite something to see the place. All these years Emile never invited me here."

"Why not?" Sheila asked.

Evette shrugged. "It was about ten years after she married Marceau, shortly after they moved here. She just..." Evette shrugged. "Quit answering my letters. Didn't pick up when I called. Eventually I gave up."

"I never knew anything about Marceau," Sheila said.

Evette smiled, staring up at the ceiling. "He was unique. You see his mark all over this property. He lived in a fantastical world, in his mind. He was wonderful. And our parents were very against him."

"Why?" Sheila sipped her wine.

"My parents were faithful—religious. Marceau was not."

"That still mattered?"

Evette smiled, but it was a sad smile. "My parents were of a different world. Call it religious. Call it superstitious. I don't really know. But they believed in many old legends and myths. They worried about Emile."

"She has dozens of books on French legends and myths in her library," Sheila said.

Evette gave a soft laugh. "Yes, that would be right there with the stories my parents told when we were young." She hesitated a moment before saying, "Marceau was a wonderful, wonderful man. They feared he would pull her from her faith and they feared for her eternal soul—you know that was a real fear in those days."

Sheila smiled.

"But they genuinely loved Marceau and feared for him, too." Evette rose abruptly. "Sheila, I'm glad I could come and see where my sister lived. I feel like an intruder. She didn't want me here. I never understood why. She and I used to be so close. I don't know why she cut me off like she did. But I feel wrong about being here."

"Mom, she left it to me. It's my home now and you're welcome here."

Evette stared at her hands on the table, manicured and laden with jewels.

"Mom, how did Marceau die? Emile was only 56 and he was gone a long time ago."

Evette shrugged. "I don't know. She just quit answering my texts and calls. I wondered if he died and she was so deep in grief…." Her voice trailed off momentarily. "I should have tried harder."

Evette stared at the table a long moment—the shiny granite table top that had belonged to her sister—before standing up abruptly. "Give me a hug," her mother said. They clung tightly for a moment before her mother pulled back and said, "I'm sure there's a reason she chose you. I just feel wrong being here. Maybe next month—maybe in two or three months. But right now, I feel this is still her home."

She glanced at the wall and suddenly smiled. Sheila followed her gaze to a wooden framed sign purchased in a gift shop somewhere. *There are more things in heaven and earth, Horatio, than are dreamt of in your philosophy. – Shakespeare*

"That sums up Emile," Evette said. "She lived in a world, in her own mind, where anything was possible, where magic and fantasy and unicorns could all be real if she just wanted them to be."

Sheila slept restlessly that night, dreaming of some mysterious creature in the forest. Her bedroom—Emile's bedroom—was mostly glass. A sliding door and large window comprised one wall. A second wall was all windows, starting only a foot off the floor and rising to a massive triangular window that lifted the bedroom ceiling to more than 15 feet. The third wall was half window.

Sheila opened her eyes, giving up on sleep. Stars twinkled in the triangular window—a beautiful view of Orion as he passed across the night sky. She loved this bedroom. She wished she had known Emile in life. Certainly the mind that created such a fantastical place was a mind that would have clicked with her own creative spirit!

But right now, all she could think about was the Beast in the forest. The glass walls opened her world to all the beauty outside. She woke every morning to the sunrise, to the beautiful trees and forest and fountain. But the glass walls also made her vulnerable.

Shivering, she got up and pulled the blind across the door that led to the deck. Pelly snuffled and lifted her head from her bed in the corner of the large room. "Yeah, I know, Girl," Sheila said. "We're going to miss the sunrise. But maybe at least I'll quit imagining something breaking through that window and get some sleep. I have an appointment in town tomorrow."

She pushed the blind open just a bit and flashed the light from her phone out across the lawn and forest. Something moved, far back in the trees. Just a tree swaying, she told herself. Or a nocturnal animal. She inched the deck door open. It was blocked by a security bar that would prevent it opening any further. Cool autumn air wafted through the three inch gap. Outside, she heard the distinct sound of a growl.

Sheila slammed the door shut and pulled the blind tight. She locked the bedroom doors and crawled under the covers, seeking respite in sleep.

Sheila sat at her nail appointment the next day, her eyes closed in the dim room where soft music played as her feet soaked in a tub. Her mother had loved to take her for mother-daughter mani-pedis and she did it now, her only real indulgence, largely because it brought back happy memories. The massage chair pummeled at her back and she sipped the red wine the salon offered.

It also seemed to help the creative process, to take the time to relax and float into her own thoughts. Some of her best stories had been concocted while relaxing in her favorite nail salon.

"It was seen again."

The words drifted into her mind. Sheila drew a deep breath, her imagination caught in the story she was editing. Something was missing. Why did the author's Sasquatch-type creature come across as comical rather than frightening? The salon worker lifted her foot out of the water, rubbing lotion up and down her legs. The creature's name, Sheila decided. The name was all wrong and ruined the whole effect. The fact it even had a name—she would suggest that to the author—was all wrong. It turned what was supposed to be frightening into a caricature, a cartoonish figure. In her mind, she could see the man-beast as it should be for the reader—terrifying.

"A wolf?" Asked a voice beside her.

"No, much bigger than a wolf. The size of...a moose maybe. But more the build of a wolf. And it growls like a wolf."

"I did hear Ed Konsky found one of his goats dead. He heard something growling out there in the night and went out with his shotgun. He saw a shadow, he said, and got himself back inside."

Sheila opened her eyes, looking at the two women across from her. They were young, both with thick, long hair, one in blonde and one in a jet black that was almost surely the result of dye. They couldn't be long out of high school.

The girl with black hair gave a little shudder and a pout of bright red lips. "I'm glad I live in town. You couldn't pay me to spend a night up by that mountain right now."

"I hope they catch it soon," the blonde girl agreed. "My boyfriend has his hunting blind out there and I'm scared for him."

Sheila scanned the thinning woods around her as she pulled slowly down the half mile of Emile's driveway—watching for any strange creature. She shut the garage door behind her car, watching the whole time that nothing crept in behind her, before getting out of her car.

Pelly wanted to go out, of course. Sheila opened the deck door in the great hall, watching as the huge black Newfie crossed the deck and wandered the broad lawn. She eyed the tree line, thinking of the faceless Ed Konsky and his goat. She regretted stopping in town for coffee after her nail appointment. The Sentinel had featured a front-page article about the thing in the woods. It seemed it was being seen most often within a mile of her own home, just south of the mountain. Dave Martin up on Mountain Drive—just half a mile from her own house—swore he'd seen it. Like a wolf, but far bigger, he said. It growled. He heard it.

"Come on, Pelly," Sheila called. "Finish up, will you?"

The dog wandered closer to the woods. Sheila drew a deep breath. If anything was there, the dog would sense it and leave, she reminded herself. Still, her insides felt tense and cold, wishing the dog would come back.

Pelly scanned the woods, then squatted, taking her sweet old time. Sheila peered into the trees. It had been days since she'd walked the wide lawn or enjoyed going close to the fountain or trickling waterfall and stream and mermaids.

Whatever it was, she told herself, would be found soon by the DNR. Life could go back to normal.

Pelly finished her business. She glanced into the forest and gave a short, sharp *woof!* Then she bolted for the deck door, bursting through and turning to look back out again. She whined.

Sheila closed the door and locked it. She turned her back to the tall, wide wall of windows to go make dinner.

The clocks ticked steadily in the background. Sheila scoured the author's 20 page short story about a beast in the forest. At the hour, the musical clock sang its song as a dozen and a half others joined in with their various chimes and jingles and lilts. Sheila clicked away at her laptop. The sun sank quickly outside, leaving her in an island of light in the great hall, surrounded by the darkness outside.

The day and the walls of glass having left the great hall warm, she had propped the two sliding doors open, blocked by bars but leaving five inches for air to get in.

On her bed, Pelly whined.

Sheila looked up. The dog shook her head and laid her nose back on her paws.

From outside came the sound of something falling—and a low growl.

Sheila jumped up, her breath coming heavily. She grabbed her phone and flashed it out the windows. It played over the treeline. Nothing moved.

"I'm just jumpy," she muttered to Pelly. *But I hope you're in for the night,* she thought.

She settled back into her arm chair in front of the big windows, resuming work on the horror story.

The clocks ticked.

Pelly heaved a heavy sigh in her bed.

The keys clacked away under Sheila's manicured fingertips.

From outside there came the distinct sound of a growl.

Sheila's head shot up and a moment later she saw the dark shape outside, hurtling toward her.

She jumped from her chair, the laptop falling to the floor as a massive shape burst through the glass windows. Glass exploded and sprinkled everywhere, a glittering rainfall.

Sheila screamed, rolling herself into a ball on the floor as glass shattered all around her. The sight of a lupine creature, yellow eyes, long fangs dripping with slather, gray matted fur, long, long legs, and snarling, and as big as a moose imprinted itself on her mind.

* * *

"Ma'am! Ma'am, are you okay? Can you hear me?"

The voice slowly cut through Sheila's consciousness. She opened her eyes. A young man stared down at her, twenty-five at most.

Sheila drew a trembling breath. She squinted into the light—it was dim, she noted. She groped with her hands, feeling a bed sheet, and turned her head, seeing flashing lights and a tall dark window on her left. "Where am I?" she murmured.

"Mercy General." The boy paused a moment. "Do you need a few minutes?"

"How...why...how am I here?" Sheila asked. "Who are you?"

"I'm the EMT who came to your house. Ryan."

Sheila's eyes slowly adjusted to the light. "How...how did you find me?" she asked.

"Someone called 911."

Sheila was silent. She tried to remember. She had curled up as the Beast crashed through the window, launching itself over her. She couldn't remember anything after that—only the spray of glass.

"My dog....?"

"The neighbors took her in. She's fine, just waiting for you to get home." Ryan tentatively took her hand. "You've very lucky. A moose breaking through a window like that...."

"It wasn't a moose," Sheila said.

"Unheard of," Ryan continued. "It was very sick. They would normally never do a thing like that."

"It wasn't a moose," Sheila murmured. Her head hurt. She was tired. She shook her head. "No. I saw it. It was a wolf. Fangs. Gray fur. It was a *wolf,* but huge." Images began to come back to her—scooting away from the thing.

"No, Ma'am." Ryan shook his head. "It was a moose."

Sheila fell back against her pillows, squeezing her eyes closed. She could see it as it came through the window—the spray of glass glittering in the lamplight and moonlight; the long, gray snout; the froth around the long, yellow fangs; the gray, matted fur. It faced her, snarling—it took a step toward her for every four she took backward, till the tall kitchen table stood between them.

The animal turned its yellow eyes to the table. The butcher knife gleamed there. Sheila considered grabbing it, defending herself. But that was impossible. She spun and threw herself through the small door into the library hallway, hurtling into the small store room at the end and crawling into a tiny crawlspace. Trembling, she managed to punch 911 into her phone, hoping Pelly had disappeared somewhere.

"Ma'am?"

She opened her eyes. "Why do you think it was a moose?" she asked. *Why hadn't the monster killed her?* It hadn't even tried to get through the flimsy wooden door.

Ryan looked at her as if the answer must be obvious. "Only something as big as a moose could have taken down that entire window and the wood frames, too."

"Isn't that...." Sheila hesitated, her head throbbing and making it hard to find the words. "Isn't that asserting the conclusion? Or affirming the consequent?" she asked. "Was there a moose in my living room?"

The thing hadn't harmed Pelly, either. Why not?

"Well—no." The man looked at her as if she was crazy. "Of course it had left."

"It just walked right back out?"

"Well, it must have, since it wasn't there."

Sheila closed her eyes and drew in a slow breath, resisting the urge toward a sarcastic comment. It wasn't there—and therefore it must have been a moose? Her head spun. "Did you find any fur?" she asked. "Wouldn't a moose have left brown fur?"

Ryan drew a sharp breath and glanced out the window with pursed lips before meeting her eyes. "As a matter of fact, there *was* a clump of gray fur caught in the remaining wood of the window."

Sheila gave him a hard stare.

"You must remember," Ryan said, as if speaking to a child, "that moose live in the forest."

"Yeah, I noticed there weren't many in New York City."

Ryan cleared his throat, ignoring her sarcasm. "It may have

scraped against a tree and picked it up or been in a fight with a wolf. It could be fur from your own dog. It could have been a gray moose—some of them are more gray."

Sheila stared at the ceiling. She'd hit her head quite hard. Was it possible she'd dreamed the strange interaction with a giant wolf? It would have killed her if it had been real. Pelly *did* have a gray patch on her. Ryan was right that any animal in the forest *might* have picked up another animal's fur. "You didn't test the fur?" she asked.

He shook his head. "Why would we? Only a moose is big enough to do that amount of damage."

"That's circular logic," Sheila whispered.

"You were pretty shaken," Ryan replied. "Understandably."

Sheila was quiet for a few moments before asking, "Why would a moose suddenly crash through a window?"

Ryan shrugged. "Maybe it was sick? Maybe the light in your house drew it? I couldn't say."

"Does this happen often around here?"

He shook his head. "Never."

"So in a never-before-heard-of event, a moose crashes through my window, then walks right back out before you get there and nobody tested the fur and there was no search done for this potentially sick animal in the woods?"

Ryan lifted his hands helplessly. "It was gone. What good would it do to look for it?"

"Well, if it's sick and crashing into people's homes maybe so it doesn't hurt anyone else?" Sheila suggested.

"I don't know," Ryan said. "I can't help you." His eyes darted from one corner of the room to another.

Sheila's eyes narrowed, watching him. "What aren't you telling me?" she asked.

He stood up abruptly. "You've had a shock. You'll be fine by tomorrow and they'll release you and send you home." He disappeared out the door, leaving her alone.

Sitting in her armchair in front of the repaired windows, Sheila turned page after page of Emile's photo albums, left on the built-in sideboard in the dining area. Emile looked very much like her sister, Evette. And ever at her side, from the time she was sixteen, was the mysterious Marceau. Turning the pages, Sheila watched him slowly age from seventeen to his mid-forties, with a touch of silver at his temples and the slightest of creases at the corners of his eyes. A handsome man full of laughter.

Sheila crossed the broad lawn, as the sun sank, to the long pen at the edge of the woods. There, the chickens clucked and rabbits scurried around. She'd bought them that morning from a nearby farmer. Sheila studied the enclosure for several minutes before looking at the latch. She unlatched it and swung the wooden door wide,.

Sunset glowed in the west, a blaze of orange on the low horizon.

Sheila sank down onto the wrought iron bench just inside the pen. She drew a deep breath, the knife clutched tight in her right hand. Her heart pounded. She had locked Pelly in the house, in the back hall shut off from all sight or sound.

The chickens and rabbits mulled around, pecking at their food, showing no inclination to leave.

Sheila closed her eyes, breathing deeply. Terror gripped her. What if she was wrong? The chickens and rabbits snuffled and pecked.

Then another sound caressed her ears: a breath drawn from a deep chest, a heavy sigh.

Sheila opened her eyes. The wolf's yellow eyes peered down into hers. It loomed, a foot above her face. Its breath was hot in her face, its fangs long and heavy.

"Trust me?" she whispered.

The wolf didn't move. Its eyes remained steady on hers.

Her knife flashed out, slicing its front leg.

Blood trickled down.

Sheila closed her eyes, her breath coming heavily, waiting…

Would its teeth clamp onto her arm, her neck?

All was silence.

Sheila opened her eyes.

A man knelt before her, looking up to her. Tears inched down his cheeks. Silver touched his temples. He bowed his head a moment before lifting his eyes to hers. "Emile could never bear to hurt me," he said. "Thank you. *Thank you!*"

Truth is Stranger than Fiction

John pulled his black SUV up in front of the old saloon and turned to his co-hosts of the wildly popular *Truth: Stranger than Fiction?* "He said he'd meet us here."

In the back seat, Greg yawned and threw his door open. "Any chance of a soda around here?"

Dan climbed out the other back door, looking around the old ghost town. He couldn't even say it looked like something out of an old western. There were several streets, rather than the stereotypical one. Far too many of the buildings were broken down. Of the signs that remained, most sagged or held on barely by a single rusty nail. A door creaked in a breeze. It did have a tumbleweed blowing down the main street. He scratched his back and yanked a baseball cap on against the glare of the sun. "Yeah, I don't think you're gonna find a cold drink here."

Mike threw open the front passenger door and stretched his long legs. "You ain't gonna find any drink here." He strolled around to the back, lifting the hatchback and pulling out his camera and tripod. "When'ja say this guy's meeting us, John?"

"He said noon."

"High noon, huh?" Dan scoffed, and yanked his baseball cap farther down over his eyes. "Building it up for an authentic feel. We got our pistols ready?" He reached into the back of the SUV for a heavy leather-bound notebook, and plopped himself into the shade of the saloon's porch, studying the notes he'd made about the place.

"So what's this Bill guy's deal?" Mike asked John. They ambled a few feet in the heat, through dust swirling around their knees. "What's he got to gain by being on our program? 'Cause you know it always starts with that."

John nodded. "He wants to open this place up as a tourist attraction. Ghosts sell. My guess is he's put together some really good stories. Has a few tricks up his sleeve. Our job is *always* to debunk if possible. Watch for these things. Start filming now before he gets here and see if you find any hidden speakers, ice machines, anything."

Mike, with his camera at the ready, rolled down the street in his Texan stride, putting a foot now and again on a step up to a porch to capture still shots of the brothel, a boarding house, and the mercantile that once sold goods to the forty-niners, miners, and homesteaders who had flooded the area in the town's hey day. A tumbleweed, as high as his knee, rolled by him, surrounded by a swirl of dust.

"Hey, Greg, can you start looking for the places we're setting up the equipment?" John asked.

"Got the map here." Greg waved a piece of paper, scanning the main street to see how it related. "The stables, upper floor of the saloon, Bootleg Hill of course."

"It's called the Rusty Nails Graveyard."

"Yeah, same, same. Back bedroom of the boarding house. Sheriff's house. Jail, hanging tree." He snorted. "Is there any place in this town that *isn't* haunted?"

"You forgot the newspaper office."

"Look out, Ghost of Jimmy Olson!" Sarcasm dripped from Dan's voice. "Here we come to find out if you're writing that article for all eternity."

"What the hell!"

They all jumped at the sound of Mike's voice from halfway down the street and looked up. He pointed the other way. They turned to see clouds of rust-red sand billowing up, as tall as a man. And through the sandy haze a man appeared.

Mike's camera shot up, filming.

The misty figure wore cowboy boots, chaps, a wide-sleeved shirt from another era, a vest, and a Stetson.

Greg scrambled behind the still-open door of the SUV, watching as the ghostly form strode forward. A big white handlebar mustache drooped down the sides of his mouth, alongside a triangular beard that would have made a Civil War general proud.

The figure burst through the billowing dusty, a tumbleweed blowing across the front of his feet and held out a hand, grinning. "You mus' be John."

John's look of shock melted into a broad smile. "And you must be Bill Nelson."

"That I am. William R. Nelson." He held out a hand.

"You like a dramatic entrance," John said, as the two men shook hands.

Bill's grin grew. "Well, now if you can make an entrance, why not make it dramatic? This is for yer teel-eh-vision after all, ain't it?" He winked, barely visible under the Stetson. "But we get plenty of them dust bowls here. Sometimes it's hard to make any other kind."

"It's great on film!" Mike said.

John gestured around the empty buildings. "Research tells us you have a lot to show us before dark falls and we start filming and recording with our equipment."

Bill led them first to the saloon. Greg moved with his EMF meter around the room as the old man spoke.

"It's Mato—Angry Bear—who still walks here today." Bill walked behind the bar, running his long fingers across the empty bottles standing in racks in front of the mirror. "These were once full. This place was once full—of laughter, of talk, of boasts." He stopped at one bottle.

Mike zoomed his camera in, filming the words *The Destroying Angel Unaged Whiskey* on the bottle where Bill's hand paused. "It was this—*the destroying angel*—that started it all."

Dan scribbled notes on his yellow legal pad, despite the fact his recorder and Mike's camera were both going.

"Mato had worked for some time with one of the town's men —Lester Proudfoot—distilling liquor. This was one of theirs. Now Lester was a quarter Sioux, so Mato trusted him. Saw them as brothers, you know?" He looked around at the four men.

Greg turned, at the momentary silence, from scanning with his EMF, and nodded his understanding.

"What happened?" John asked quietly.

"It was June 6, 1890. Mato found out Lester was selling the whiskey to the saloon in the next town for twice what he told Mato he was—cheating Mato out of fair payment."

John, sitting at one of the tables, watched quietly as Bill lifted the bottle from its rack. Liquid still shone in the bottom.

Dan's pen stilled over his legal pad.

"Mato came in one day, confronting Lester as he talked with Amos, the saloon owner, over the bar. Yelling and shouting. All the men gambling here that day—it all stopped. People starin,' waitin' to see what would happen. The ladies backing up to the stairs, wantin' to be away from whatever was to come." Bill stared up into a corner of the saloon's ceiling. "Demanding he be given his fair due. Lester spun on him, pulled a gun."

"Shot him in cold blood?" Greg almost gasped. His EMF fell to his side, forgotten in his hand.

Bill chuckled. "Not quite how it happened. Y' see, Pen Watts, Mato's friend, came bursting through the door. He was the town wit—he and Rusty Nels—the jovial one who just wanted everyone to get along. He told Lester, 'Put down the gun. Come on now—do what's right. It's just money, aye? Mato did his work, give him his pay.'"

"And?" John asked.

Mike trained his camera on the old man with his heavy mustache and triangular beard.

"And things got out of hand. Lester aimed his gun at Pen and Pen fired back. But Jack Miles, one of the miners who was gamblin' that day—maybe it was 'cause he had some prejudice in him, on account of his family was killed by the Sioux. Or maybe he just didn't want to see a man die that day. But Jack threw himself at Pen and the bullet went where it was never intended and Jack saw a man die all the same."

"Who died?" Dan asked.

Bill stared at the scarred wooden floor behind the bar. "Mato. The bullet hit Mato. June 6, 1890 They were friends. And now Pen had killed Mato."

He laughed suddenly, unscrewing the bottle, and raising it high. "Here's to you, Mato! Cheers! Sloncha! Prost!" And he gulped down all that remained in the bottle. "You were a good man!"

"How old is that stuff?" Greg asked. "Is that safe to drink?"

"It gets better with age," Dan said. "I mean, I think it does."

"Yeah, wish I'd known about that when we got here. I could have used a drink—of anything."

"Here's to spirits!" Bill raised the bottle and took a second swallow, before laughing with gusto. "Those in the bottle and those in the town!"

Mike's camera closed in on Bill's face, then panned to Dan who laughed and raised his own imaginary bottle. "To spirits in the bottle and the spirits in town!" he echoed.

Bill led them through a number of the buildings. In the livery he told of the fire of 1891. March 15. Jed, the groom, tried to lead the horses out as the stable burned. He succumbed to the smoke, dying as the very last horse was led out. His wife fell at her knees beside him, cursing the last horse. "Was the horse more important than you being here for your children!" she raged.

Mike's mind spun with ways to re-create the scene as he filmed the new stable built in place of that which had burned, considering which actors and actresses he might use.

Bill stared solemnly at the floor just inside the stables. He shook his head. "Six children he had, and one on the way."

"What happened to the wife?" Greg asked.

Bill looked up, blinking as if surprised to see them. Then he grinned. "She married Rusty Nels. He took those kids on like they were his own and there were five more and it was a house full of jokes and laughter and tall tales told, wonderful stories woven. The kids often said—'If only Papa could stay here forever telling his stories and making people happy like he does us.'" He winked. "Nothing better'n a good tale!"

He led them down another street, stopping to point out where the Reverend Thompson had preached and taken care of orphans in the white wooden church, and where years later the Reverend Tucker had preached and on a Saturday night held great revival meetings with singing and dancing; the smithy where Rusty Nels and Sara Smith Nels and their twelve children had lived; the schoolhouse where the aging Miss Violet had finally met and married the widowed Judge Hastings.

"Just how old was she?" Dan asked.

"Oh, twenty-three already," Bill said soberly. "The town thought she was a spinster for life."

"Does one of them still haunt the place?"

"Neither of them." Bill climbed the stairs to the judge's home —now a sad empty shell of what had once been a regal house.

Faded wallpaper clung to the walls. A hole gaped in the top of one window.

The four men followed Bill up the stairs and into the room where he stopped. "But their nanny, now. She can't rest." He pointed to the crib standing in one corner, a shabby, moth-eaten blanket laid out in it. "She was on duty the night the baby died. Little Ellen Lenore. Seven months old. Hardly poor Josephine's fault."

"Why can't she rest, then?" John asked.

Mike moved around the room, filming it, his mind creating the scene and just how he'd fill modern actresses into the room. He had an image of Josephine. Mattie Howe would be perfect to play her.

"People often blame themselves when they shouldn't," Bill said. He rested a hand on the dusty rail of the crib, then laughed. "And those who *should* blame themselves, usually don't."

"What did the baby die of?" Greg asked. He peered into the crib.

"She took sick," Bill answered. "Babies often took sick in those days. Got a fever and died. No one could have saved her. Doc couldn't save her. Poor Violet was never the same afterward and Josephine blamed herself. Just the sort of girl she was, always blaming herself. So she took poison."

"She killed herself over it?" John asked in disbelief.

"Sad waste of a life," Bill said. "She was only 18. Let's go on to the Rusty Nails."

They trooped after him back, out of the stifling stuffiness of Judge Hasting's house into the glaring, stifling heat of the day.

Sweat dripped down John's back as he followed Bill up the hill to the cemetery.

Mike's camera whirred at the graveyard as Dan scribbled notes while Bill told them of its history. "The first major catastrophe in the town. The mine collapsed, killed a dozen men.

Men with wives, children. Dustin Moray had a wife back east in Ohio, waiting on his word and pregnant with their third child."

"Why was it called Rusty Nails?" John asked.

"Because it's where Rusty Nels was buried." Bill held his Stetson to his chest, gazing at the ramshackle tombstones, all atilt.

"Rusty Nels—Rusty Nails!" Greg said. "I get it!"

Bill laughed. "Aye. A joke Rusty himself would have liked. He'd a sense of humor."

"But if the mine collapsed, weren't the dozen men buried here, too? Why not after one of them?"

"Because when it happened, when the church bells started ringing and a lone man came running to shout the news, Rusty was the first one on the scene." Bill jammed his hat back on his head. "He was 68—but still strong from a lifetime of working the smithy. He dove in there and started hauling men out. If he'd not been there, it would've been three dozen men or more who died. He led the charge, got others to help, and he went in time after time, almost single-handedly lifting beams off men, or dragging out those with broken legs or cracked ribs or who'd been knocked out cold, who couldn't get themselves out."

"Wow!" Greg said.

"So he died down there?"

"He died a week later from inhaling the air down there." Bill led the men to a large Celtic cross in the middle of the cemetery. It was cleaner than the rest. Bill held his Stetson to his chest, grinning, as the four ghost-hunters filmed the faded words: *I always knew minors would be the death of me!*

"They misspelled miners," Greg said.

Bill laughed. "Rusty played banjo. He always joked about not wanting to play minor songs. They're the sad ones. He liked to laugh."

Dan chuckled. "Funny."

"He was the guy with all the kids?" Greg asked. "The kids who said he should stay forever making people laugh?"

Bill grinned. "That's the one."

"Well, he just gave me a laugh 150 years later," Dan said.

"Even in death he had a sense of humor," Mike said. He moved his camera past the long row of smaller tombstones stretched all around Rusty Nels, panning Sarah Smith Nels, and the twelve sons and daughters, the Smiths and the Nels and Irene Smith Hughes.

Bill stopped at one that read Myrtle Nels Down. "That's enough of a downer!" he said brightly. "Let's go see the Hanging Tree!"

Through the rest of the afternoon, Bill told them a myriad of stories. There was the Hanging Tree—where Young Weston was hanged for armed robbery. He was captured three months after the robbery by a posse. Now, he roamed between the Hanging Tree and the bank. At night, the sound of gold jingling in a bag could be heard.

In the newspaper office, Mike filmed the typewriter that was said to be heard clicking on many a night.

"Heard by who?" Greg asked. "There's nobody here."

"Back when people were still here," Bill said. "And there will be people again when I finish the necessary repairs and open this town up for tours and for people to stay in some of these old buildings." He ran his hand over the keys of the old-fashioned typewriter. "The editor of the paper, Albert Gross, ran an article about the mayor, Phineas Young, suggesting he had might possibly been seen too near the brothel. And Phineas married to a good Christian woman and attending service every Sunday."

Dan scribbled on his yellow legal pad.

Mike filmed.

Greg drew in a deep breath.

"It came to a fight?" John asked.

"A fight indeed," Bill said. He laughed suddenly. "Never a dull moment in this old town! It was a place of self-made men, the kind who got by, by fighting for themselves, not by backing down. They went at it in the newspaper office that day and it came to grappling, wrestling, and Mayor Phineas was thrown to the ground. He shoulda known better than to take on Al. He dashed his head against a desk and within 24 hours, he was dead."

"Why does he haunt the newspaper office, if he was the mayor?" John asked.

Bill shrugged. "My guess—because it's where he died. But more..." He looked around, meeting the eyes of each of the four ghost hunters. "...because he knows what was said about him in that paper was true. He's in his place of truth for all eternity—unless he faces his guilt and admits it."

He took them next to a boarding house where a woman in 19th century garb roamed the halls by night, calling the name of the husband she shot, begging his forgiveness, knowing only now in death that her accusations of adultery were wrong, seeking to un-do what she did in 1893.

Bill led them at last back to the saloon.

They settled around a weathered table, scarred with knife blades, water stains, and burns. No doubt it had its share of stories, even apart from Mad Old Marty who had died here over a winning hand of poker.

"You bring it to life," John said. "How do you know so much about the people who lived here?"

"Research. This town is my passion and I want their stories to live on. They were real people."

"You didn't make these stories up as a way to bring in business?" John asked. "Can you verify all these people?"

Bill grinned at them. "That's your job, ain't it? You do your research and you'll find all these people lived exactly as I've told you. Plus, I expect you'll encounter at least a few of them tonight. They were a lively bunch."

Bill took a bottle of spirits from behind the counter, and several glasses. He filled them with amber liquid and the men all raised their glasses to one another, clinking, and smiling with their success. All around, the golden liquid went down throats and glasses hit the scarred table.

"So let's say it's all true," John said, "Why do you think ghosts—or spirits, or souls—stay around?" He took a second drink of the brandy Bill had poured.

In two corners, Mike's cameras watched the table. Mike himself jumped from the table to zoom in on Bill's face with his own camera.

"Well, that's always the question," Bill said. He stared a moment at the amber remaining in his low ball before lifting his eyes to John's and saying, "And I think there are different reasons, dependin' on who the spirit is." He lifted his glass. "Prost! To spirits!"

John clinked his glass to Bill's and downed more of the brandy before saying, "And what are those reasons?"

Bill set the glass down and stared at the empty, cob-webbed bottles lining the saloon's mirror. "Some are caught through regret or tryin' to repent of what they did. Some are still denyin' they're dead—won't accept it and they think the livin' who comes through is still of their world. They're confused." He stared into the mirror.

Mike turned his camera slowly, following the direction of Russell's look.

"Others?" John prompted.

"Others," Bill said, "are here on the Lord's business."

"Meaning what?" Greg asked. He glanced at Dan, who fiddled with his small hand-held detector.

"They're here to warn the livin.' They see someone about to fall down a well, say, and they stop 'em. They died in a fire and now they protect the house from ever burnin' down again, or their ancestors from ever dyin' in a fire. It's what they've chosen."

Dan looked up from his instrument. "So caught in guilt or staying to protect?"

"There's one other reason they stay behind." Bill leaned across the table, his eyes alight.

"What's that?" John held a pen at the ready over his notebook, while Mike circled the table slowly, training his camera on Bill, capturing him from the front.

"For fun!'" Bill grinned broadly.

"*Fun?*" Greg asked in disbelief. "I've never heard that one before. Why would it be *fun* to haunt a place?"

"Fun for the livin,'" Bill said, a gleam in his eye. "Think about the stories you tell!"

"We report what's here. We're investigators just trying to understand what's real and what isn't," John replied.

"Ah, but you go in dis-believing, yes?"

John shrugged. "I think most things can be explained by science. I think people fear what they don't understand, but if they understood, they'd realize there's nothing out of the ordinary. It's why I do the show—to show people not to be gullible."

"Have you ever found one you can't explain away?"

John twisted his glass slowly between his fingers, studying Bill's face. "There are some I can't explain a hundred percent. But most of them, I have a pretty good idea how it's done."

Bill lifted the bottle and tilted it into John's glass. He set it down before saying, "What's the most interesting story of your life?"

John lifted his glass swirling it a bit, studying its amber depths. Finally he looked up. "I don't know. Graduating from college. White water rafting."

Bill waved a hand. "Lots of people do that."

"I threw up on a roller coaster once," Mike offered.

Bill shook his head, rolling his eyes. "That's the most fascinating thing that's ever happened to you? Is that the story you'll tell over a campfire? The story you'll tell to friends over a private dinner? The story you'll tell your grandchildren?"

John watched Bill. The man's eyes glowed, golden brown with bright spots of yellow in them. For just a moment, in the evening light of the saloon, it seemed only his mustache and beard showed, bright white against the dim interior. John blinked.

Bill beamed at him. "You have no Great Story, do you?"

John shook his head. Even winning the high school baseball tournament, that last slide into home plate, didn't seem to be what Bill was talking about.

Bill swirled the liquid in his glass, then pierced John's eyes with his own. "What if," he said, "some souls hang around earth to give A Story to others? To put some mystery and magic into the lives of those still living?"

"I don't get it," Greg said. "What would be the point?"

Bill turned his eyes on Greg. "What is *your* Great Story?" he asked.

Dan stared back, one eyebrow drawn down. "I took the homecoming queen to prom—that was kinda cool. I went to this rally once in college...."

"Who *hasn't* done those things?" Bill asked.

Dan bristled. "Well, lots of guys would have liked to take her...."

"Does it make you think?" Bill asked. "Does it draw your mind back over and over asking, *What happened,* and make you think about what life really is?"

Dan laughed—albeit half-heartedly. "Life was pretty good that night."

"I took a girl on a date!" Bill laughed out loud. "Is that the story that changed your life? Made you re-think all you thought you knew? Is that the story that will make you think about life, the universe, and all that surrounds us? Make you wonder about this world that we're living in?"

"I really don't get it," Greg said.

Mike focused his camera on Bill.

Bill stood up. He raised his amber glass in the air, saying, "Gentlemen! To the stories that feed our imaginations! The stories that change us. The stories that stay with us. The stories that make life interesting, that open our minds to mystery, magic and wonder!" He drank his glass down, grinned broadly as he wiped a hand across his mouth and slapped the glass down on the table. "I believe some of these spirits stay out of a sense of fun, a sense of mystery—they're staying for *your* sake! To give you a moment of wonder, a chance to step outside your ordinary world, a mystery and bit of magic you'll never forget, a memory that forevermore makes you think—*What is beyond this world?*"

He slapped the glass on the table and looking around at each one of them, said, "Because that—the moment you ask, *What is beyond this world*, that is the moment that changes your life. Because you begin to think about how you're living. It's the moment you *begin* living!"

The camera whirred.

Bill doffed his Stetson suddenly, winking, and added, "And who does not want a bit of mysteriousness and magic in his life? We all want...." He paused dramatically before adding, "A *Story!* We all want that moment so out of the ordinary, that we can tell it forever over campfires and to our grandchildren." He bowed low, before rising and placing the Stetson back on his head. "That, Boys, is why some souls continue to wander this earth."

"I don't get it," Greg said again.

Bill laughed out loud, his head lifted to the ceiling, before looking Dan in the eye. "We're having fun." He dropped his hands to the table, piercing Dan with his look before moving his eyes to John. "*We're...having...fun!* We're giving *you* fun!"

John stared at Bill. An uncomfortable idea formed in his mind. "Do you go by....?"

"William. Russell. Nelson." Bill winked. "Have a beautiful and mysteriously wonderful day, Gentleman. Think about all that's out there in the world!" He turned and headed out of the saloon, the half-doors swinging behind him.

Mike followed him hastily, filming him as he disappeared, a wraith, into the sand billowing at dusk in Triamin's streets.

~ ~ ~ ~ ~

"It's not possible." John muttered it for the eighth time. "Start from the beginning."

"We're going to see the same thing," Mike objected.

"No, it's not possible," John said more forcefully.

With a shrug, Mike skipped to the beginning. His camera captured the three of them, John, Greg, and Dan, staring into a billow of dust; talking to the rising sun; walking through the jail talking to someone who didn't exist on the film.

Only at the grave site of Rusty Nels did the camera show a man of 60 with a drooping white mustache and triangular beard, in cowboy boots, chaps, and a Stetson.

In the saloon, John, Dan, and Greg drank from their low balls, having a conversation that seemed as if it missed some part, as if, perhaps, they'd had too much to drink and made no sense amongst themselves.

Mike clicked off the computer.

Dan tapped with agitation into his laptop, searching the town and the names of Bill Nelson and Rusty Nels.

"William Russell Nelson," he said finally. "Bill Nelson. He went by Rusty and they shortened Nelson to Nels. Rusty Nails."

The two of them sat silently for a full minute. Shock sat heavily on John's shoulders.

Mike shifted in his chair and rose. He paced the room once, twice, before stopping and saying, "Do you have a story now?"

John smiled. The grin grew, and suddenly, he burst out laughing. "I have a story!"

The Burning and the Spirit

By Chris R. Powell

As with all peoples through history, there are legends and stories which mix the normal with the super-normal. Such mixing is done to explain, and to highlight the morals which frame the long-term success of a people. Actions have consequences, whether good or bad. If we frame these actions in universal terms, we teach and learn, in contrast to merely witnessing. In this story, I have brought together several Cherokee legends and lessons, both to honor the Cherokee and to explain that values across time have common foundation.

Junaluska scanned the eastern horizon at sunrise. Something wasn't right. The sky did not have its normal azure hue, but rather seemed gray or even brown in tone. Despite his young 17 years, he had seen this before, and it was a harbinger of death and disease. He smelled the air, tasting its tang of smoke and garbage — just a note, but enough to know what was on the way, perhaps a day or so out.

Danuwoa focused down on his prey—a beautiful stag, with a proud look and the confidence of an animal that had evaded conquer before. The stag is the king of the forest, and here was the king of kings, protecting all other creatures; an animal of power! Danuwoa sought to transfer this power to himself—to learn its message, and also complement his own power with this totem of sensitivity, intuition, and gentleness. On this path was his future as Chief of the Anikawi—balancing power, protection, and guidance from the spirits of the forest and its creatures.

He knew the Meesink story from his distant Lenape relatives through the Elders. Meesink spoke for all, asking The Creator not to make man. They would dig the earth and pollute the rivers. We will have a contest to determine the wisdom of creating man, the Creator said. If I can move the mountain, I will make man. If you can move the mountain, I will not.

The Creator won, smashing Meesink in the head with the mountain, affirming the Creator's wisdom and allowing the creation of man.

Yes, man would dig the ground and pollute the rivers, but he would also tend to the deer and appreciate their spirit—use every part, for bedding, for food, for hunting, for clothing. Messink had done as he'd promised the Creator, helping man tend to and hunt the deer, and now Danuwoa would be true to the spirit of the earth and land, and take this animal's spirit into his own.

Junaluska focused on his own pursuit, on the east, thinking too, on his fate. He had been named for the great Chief who saved Andrew Jackson's life in his victory over the Creeks at Horseshoe Bend in 1814, but, he thought, he seemed destined, rather than live up to that great Chief, to live down to the meaning of the name—*one who tried and failed, and keeps failing.*

No matter what he did, he could not seem to do the right thing. Desires burned within him, but seemed to flicker and fail, like a flame in the breeze, every time. As a strong young man, he had knowledge of fighting, hunting, and of the spirits of forest and animal. As a headstrong young man with little knowledge of his fellow man, he got himself into the trouble that comes to those with strength but not temperance. His attempts at short cuts were usually met with what the wiser members of the tribe knew came from sloth—the spirits in the forest would act in their own way, tripping, pushing arrows away from their targets, crunching leaves loudly underfoot rather than let one silently pass through the forest, all the while mocking from afar.

"It is the spirit's way to guide you," the old shaman had told him. "Not just to what you want, but to do so in the right way."

"No matter what I do," Junaluska had protested, "I fail and I am mocked."

The old man chuckled. "Yes, they will laugh and continue poking if you keep getting it wrong. Junaluska indeed—the one who tries, the one who fails. The one who burns inside..."

Winter's late afternoon began its descent into evening as the stag chewed silently on leaves and the few remaining dried berries. He warily scanned to his left, and to his right, lifting his front leg to be ready to bolt at a moment's inclination. His flank rippled in muscle as this legacy of Meesink took his place between the Creator and man, leading his herd with justice and mercy.

On the stag's chest, Danuwoa saw the scars of confrontation with lesser bucks who had tried to usurp their leader and protector. They had been, Danuwoa, could guess, quickly moved to their correct position in the herd. The stag had taught the bucks well—letting them get their horns wet with a bit of his blood, but, in the end, showing them what they were and what they were not. Danuwoa's arms and legs bore similar marks of courage and victory in battle. Arrows had penetrated but not found their mark; knives had been wielded and their holders rendered quickly powerless before their fate became clear—Danuwoa would see their spirits onward to the next life, and he would live to fight another day. His reputation was growing in the tribe, and the Elders were pleased. They had named him well. He truly was the Warrior.

Januluska had crossed paths with Danuwoa a time or two, and come out the worse for it, only increasing the burning within him. Despite his youth and strength, Junaluska could never get the better of Danuwoa—every parry and thrust of fist and arm during their wrestling matches was always met with a notch more force and balance from the Warrior.

Every brave counted. Danuwoa wanted this impulsive youth at his side—but in the right way. So he taught Januluska as the stag taught the bucks—a fist might hit home, but never with lethality. A moment's apparent domination was quickly met with a flip and pin. Junaluska could never see that this was teaching and not mocking, and again his spirit burned like a hot flame within him. Because of his impatience and failure to strategize on the hunt or in battle, Danuwoa kept Januluska on the edge of battle so as not to disadvantage the whole. Junaluska took it as an affront, raging at Danuwoa more than once, in front of the tribe.

The Elders' smiles faded when they saw Januluska—they knew that they had named him correctly, and Januluska knew they knew. He so wanted to transcend his name and live up to his namesake Chief, but he kept doing it in the wrong way.

The US Army camped 10 miles to the east of Januluska's position in the forest. As with all such modern forces, they came with a tang in the air—of sweat, gunpowder, blood, fire smoke, and burning garbage. They brought with them the diseases of the old world—smallpox, plague, and consumption. The rats ran before them, to ready the forces' arrival at their next camp—to raid their stashes of food, raid their middens, and raid their tents, feasting on grain and even flesh, spreading their awfulness. Death, too, traveled with the army—taking the creatures of the forest, in numbers that seemed greater than the soldier's need, and stalking the people of the forest and plains. Their blood ran, like the rivers of the earth, as they succumbed to superior battle tactics and weapons.

The Cherokee determined they would erase the presence of this noxious people from the land when they got the chance. They would do it with the lust of battle and destruction in their hearts, rapaciously slaughtering when they could. Thus the battles went, back and forth, and yet the Army continued their advance as time passed. The Cherokee were being displaced, the forest cut down and replaced with farm land.

The creatures of the forest also ran before these people and the Cherokee must follow their sustenance, in spirit and in stomach. The blood of the earth, the rivers and lakes, became fouled by runoff from the settlements, passing on disease and death in their own way.

And yet, for the Cherokee, there were also benefits, including better weapons for hunting, whether animals or other tribes, better cloth for clothing, and liquor for the addling of mind—which sometimes was not a bad idea as the Cherokee warrior contemplated their dislocation and constant movement. Forgetting one's woes in a bottle of whiskey postponed the day of reckoning and loss one more time.

It sometimes felt as if even the powerful spirits of legend and forest were leaving the Cherokee people, as every battle with the Army or with the settlements seemed to go more poorly, despite the tribes' occasional victories.

Januluska had made his own deal with Tsul'Kalu, the great lord of the game, or, as the Army and settlements called him—the Devil.

The Army had taken their position on Januluska's word as they worked to relocate a broad swath of Cherokee people from North and South Carolina west to Tennessee, and farther west still into Oklahoma where settlement was sparse and foreign to the Cherokee. It lacked the forests and rolling mountains of the east, and the great variety of game. There were bison, yes, but Cherokee hunting methods were not suited to these large behemoths and the meat was smelly and abhorrent to their appetites—not smooth and delicious, like the meat of the buck and stag, which seemed to move right to Cherokee muscle and mind, transferring the innate nature of the deer to the warrior, fueling his ability to protect both his people and their land.

Yet more Cherokee were being moved every month and year, and now the Army was here, bribing Januluska and those of his ilk with faint promises and perhaps a bottle of whiskey.

Januluska had given up the position of the tribe, secluded as they were on a river bend, to the Army, and they were now just a day away. Watching the smoke rise from their camp, Januluska smiled. Danuwoa would finally learn who was more powerful and better than he, and perhaps the Army would even kill him in battle, leaving Januluska as the winner in their ongoing ritual of strength, finally.

His spirit burned within, burning impure and red-hot, and not with the pure white-hot fight of battle and quarry, not in alignment with the spirit of the Creator, or Meesink, or the spirits in forest and fauna, when their energy flowed through man's veins as the rivers flowed across the land.

No, this red burning was that of retaliation, of pridefulness, and of rage.

The red flame has burned hosts and victims throughout time, leading to a path of dishonor. As with all dishonor, the casualties would mount, afflicting not just the impetuous one, but the tribe and forest around him. As with all such casualties, their number and their affliction would be unknown to the red flame's host, and if known would only compound the anger, rage, and dishonor. What would be the consequence of Januluska's dishonor and impure heart?

Danuwoa felt a flash in his heart and mind. Something was wrong, but he couldn't put his finger on it. The spirits of forest and animal had spoken to him, but he did not directly perceive their message. He continued his concentration on the stag, which seemed to him to get a touch less wary, and therein lay Danuwoa's victory: By patience and by reaching the stag's spirit and making it part of his own. Indeed, the stag looked his way, and their eyes met. The stag did not flee. It paused in its eating, and Danuwoa felt its wisdom and purity.

The stag also had felt the tears of the land that was behind the flash Danuwoa felt, and it seemed to say that Danuwoa should listen, and listen more closely. Danuwoa felt the pull of spirit and land—these forces were gathering strength in him, and he was becoming more aware of what the land, waters, and sky could and would tell you if you gave them your heart, mind, ears, eyes, and your senses of touch and smell.

He wondered if he should return home or continue his hunt. In the moment's indecision, the stag bolted into the forest, fleeing quickly beyond the range of Danuwoa's bow. A flash of anger at the lost opportunity hit him. It was quickly replaced by contemplation on what this message from the stag was. Danuwoa knelt in the forest, listening to what everything and everyone around him was saying. The tang of smoke and disease crept into his nostrils, and the flash of the forest's spirit was replaced by a sense of dread. He had smelled this before.

The day passed. Danuwoa continued his hunt—for the stag, yes, but also for whatever his quarry could be. A warrior did not stand on the principle of only hunting the best. At the right time, if the Creator willed it, the stag would be his goal. Today, it might be a rabbit, or even a turtle. All fueled the people in their own way, each communicating their spirit and sense. He continued his journey through the forest, finally returning home with no game. His continued contemplation of what the stag and forest had told him caused his aim and concentration to be off. Even the rabbit had mocked him.

Something was wrong.

Januluska watched from the edge of the forest the next day as the Army arrived at the river bend. They moved with a zeal that was not ordinary for this dirty people—it resembled the passion and energy of his own people in battle. Where would this power and force come from in this Army? It didn't make sense.

As he watched, the Army bore down on the settlement, surprising the tribe. Warriors raced out, trying to fight, but they were at every disadvantage. The Army quickly surrounded the tribe, and began, not a relocation, but a slaughter—capturing some, but shooting many as the warriors attempted to meet gun with bow and knife.

From his hiding place, Januluska sought his fifteen-year-old sister's tent. He had sent the Army only to relocate, not to slaughter! He saw her try to flee. Two soldiers caught her, pushing her back in and the flap fell. The heat rose in Januluska's chest and face. Their aim was not to relocate or even to kill—but to mark her for life, to dishonor her.

He knew as if he was there. As the soldiers muffled her screams, her spirit flowed from her, replaced by greyness and death. She would be forever lost, in spirit as well as her life's mission.

The red flame of Januluska's rage had claimed more than just the tribe—the casualties continued to mount. His sister, Ahyoka, she who brought happiness, was now a shell of herself.

Danuwoa fought bravely but was eventually captured by the Army. The Army soldiers who finally caught him hacked his right hand off in retaliation for having cut down several of their unit. While Danuwoa wrapped hide and cloth around what was left of his arm, not giving any outward appearance of pain or shame, he saw two things from the corner of his eye. On the one side, he saw Januluska on the edge of the forest, not fighting, just sitting, and on the other, he saw Januluska's sister emerge from her tent, bloodied and her face drained of all color and spirit.

Januluska saw what had happened to Danuwoa and smiled in glee, and then saw his sister, and his heart practically stopped.

After the battle, what was left of the tribe was gathered into a clearing, stripped of their possessions, homes, and weapons, and readied for the long march west. Danuwoa was fierce in his determination, and yet, sat, powerless against this Army.

Januluska himself had been captured from the forest. The Army unit here was not the one he had made his deal with, and didn't care that he was supposed to be spared. To the commanding Captain, Cherokee were Cherokee, and Cherokee must go west.

Ahyoka sat wrapped in on herself, still in the clothing from that fateful, awful encounter, with little sympathy from the women of the tribe, sitting in a limbo between having been dishonored and being the one who dishonored. In a bitter way, the tribe considered such a victim to have brought shame on the tribe, and that it would have been better to be dead, with the Creator, rather than living out life in this world, reminding everyone around her what the Army had done to them symbolically as well as physically. This only increased their shame, and hers. Ahyoka's spirit was indeed far from her. Januluska felt this as well. He knew his red flame had brought far more trouble than he had meant. He tried to sit near his sister, but the wall between them was great.

The Elders met near one side of the group. They were grim in their determination. Januluska was summoned to the center of the circle. The Army guarded, watching from a short distance; but the tribe's customs were their own, and the Army did not interfere. They coated Januluska in pitch, and covered him in ashes and the detritus from the midden. He had brought shame on his entire people, the tribe, and his sister, and he would pay by literally having the ends of his deeds stuck to him as his anger at Danuwoa had stuck within his heart.

At night, while the Army was paying less attention, Januluska was banished from the tribe into the forest with no clothing and no provisions. He would forever be on his own, apart from his people and their support.

If he survived, it would only be through his own repentance and atonement to the Creator—and if the Creator in his mercy granted him ability to survive on his own a world and elements that called for a tribe working together to protect and aid one another.

If he did not survive, his spirit would be forever maligned, in legend, and in truth. The Creator would deal with him—he was beyond the tribe now.

The Elders renamed Januluska's sister Tanamara—*the lonely wind*. She would continue to ride this lonely wind, not speaking, barely able to close her eyes, always staring into the gap of night with overwhelming loss and lack of spirit. She walked westward with the tribe, but largely behind her people. The wind across the prairie was lonely indeed, and she personified it.

The Army soon found Januluska, practically frozen—in spirit as well as body, his face as blank and spiritless as Tanamara's. This Army unit recognized Januluska as the one who had betrayed his tribe's position and hung him for escape. Januluska breathed his last not with a fighting spirit, resisting the rope, but with resignation. His neck snapped not like a warrior's, with resounding strength, but like a rabbit's, weak and green. His last breath came out like a rabbit's as well—with a mute, mewling whine.

As his spirit departed him, Tsul'Kalu was there, smiling his merciless smile. The Elders had made their own deal with Tsul'Kalu in his eternal role as Evil's companion. To Evil you go if through Evil you came, and this agent of spiritual death was always available to any who consulted him.

Tsul'Kalu pronounced the fate of Jaluluska's spirit: It would walk between this world and the next, never advancing, always in pain, always distant from the Creator, and Meesink, and anything else true and good in the spirit world. He would see the spirit world, and only ever appreciate it in the stink of his own deeds and shame, as the pang from the red flame of his anger would never leave him but waft into his spirit-nostrils, always burning, always scarring.

Danuwoa sat with Tanamara, and told her what her brother had done. Tanamara nodded her head, having seen Januluska's spirit in her dreams. She could not forgive him for what had happened to her. Her shame was connected to him in a way that could not be transcended. As she walked this earth and her brother walked between this world and the next, the reminders would always be there. She could not marry, she could not ever honor her tribe. She would always be the product of her shame.

The following day, Tanamara hung herself.

Tsul'Kalu was there waiting, having obtained from Januluska more bounty on his awful deeds. Suicide dishonors the tribe and one's spirit. She was tied to her brother's spiritual limbo and journey, but only as a further affliction to his spirit, always reminding him of her horror and shame.

To this day, one or both can be seen, usually as an omen or harbinger of spiritual lament and toil, similar to the perpetual journey both of these spirits are on as they forever walk the boundary between this world and the next. The Cherokee have a legend about one's spirit joining the Milky Way on its starry path. Tanamara and Januluska will never be there. They can only watch as the dead walk their path to the light. They can only watch as the living do good or bad on their own daily paths. They do have the power to reach into this world and show themselves for what they are, but it has been so long since they died that few know of their provenance and are merely scared or confused by what they see, which only exacerbates the difficulty and awfulness of their state. The Cherokee remember their journey as a lesson in loyalty, trust, aligning one's actions with the Creator, and the consequences of not having any of this.

A hundred years later, Bud Gaspard walked with his girl, Colleen, in Ft. Leonardwood, Missouri. They ran, laughing, through the woods to the deep underground springs there, where native peoples said a portal opens to the underworld. Evening turned to night as they sat on a bench near the springs, listening to the muffled lapping of water on the large stones and cave nearby. As clouds began to cover the moon and darkness hemmed in around them, Bud and Colleen glanced up the hill to the building there—some kind of garage, with a single weak light burning on a pole above it.

Bud wasn't sure, but he saw something. It looked like an 8-foot tall bowling pin, fully black, near another, similar specter, fully grey, both of them inky, oily in sheen. They seemed to suck away all the light near them, turning it to darkness.

The specters drifted slowly through the brush near the garage, and then turned, moving toward the couple, who sat transfixed and frozen despite their increasing shock and desire to flee.

The specters drew so close as to touch them, to half draw their spirits were drawn from them.

As Bud and Colleen stared at the strange beings, the movies of their lives seemed to play within the specters—his on the black one, and hers on the grey one. Their eyes were fixed open, unblinking, floating in a sense of compulsion and fate, and yet of choice. As with other such legends and stories, the stories they watched were perhaps not guaranteed fate, and yet, forces would ensure deliverance to Tsul'Kalu if their paths were maintained.

Colleen slumped suddenly onto Bud's shoulder and Bud sagged to the ground. They fell into a trance-like sleep beside the spring.

Bud and Colleen woke near dawn. They glanced sheepishly at one another. "You saw them?" he asked.

Colleen nodded and gave a small shudder. "I feel like something happened. I mean besides just seeing them. But I can't remember what it was."

"A bad dream," Bud said. But he didn't sound as if he believed it. A sense of foreboding clung to him. Colleen looked equally disturbed.

"Let's get out of here," she said.

As they turned to walk on the path, they glanced back towards the spring and thought they caught a glimpse of the black and grey figures, but the couple did not recognize them. They broke into a run, racing to escape the woods.

That night, they partied with friends. A little too much beer, a little too much Jagermeister. Bud and Colleen stumbled into their car, laughing at a joke that would be far less funny without the beer. As Bud turned the key in the ignition, he looked in the rearview mirror. It was just a flash, but he thought he saw something. He looked harder. Nothing was there.

"Too much beer!" Colleen laughed and punched his shoulder.

Bud shrugged his shoulders and started the car, puling out onto the road. He oversteered back and forth a bit, he and Colleen laughing as he found his place in his lane.

A young family drove in a minivan on the other side, as Bud's car drifted in the lane.

Tsul'Kalu sat in the back seat, smiling.

Excerpts from *The Saint in the Cellar*

The Saint in the Cellar *started long ago when we looked at a house on St. Paul's historic Summit Hill, just down from the Cathedral. The house and ruins as described here, exist, including Anthony's cell—with only minor differences due to faulty memory. Such an odd thing as finding a grated, paneled cell immediately called to mind the anchorites, whom we knew from my research for the Blue Bells Chronicles. The Saint in the Cellar was born!*

While many people will not regard a story about a saint to be paranormal or supernatural it is, like the others, a question of what is beyond the world we see. Anthony has his own mysteries.

JACOB

God's will be done.

Jacob seemed to hear the words as if they came from his wall. It wasn't the first time. It didn't happen often, but it happened again.

"Mama?" he asked, from his bedroom down the hall from the kitchen.

"Yes, dear?"

"What does it mean for God's will to be done? Why do we say that in church?"

"Come to dinner, Jacob. Wash your hands first."

"But, Mama? What is God's will?"

"Later, dear – get those hands washed!"

"Yes, Mama."

Jacob went to the bathroom across from his room and turned on the faucet. The water ran down from the faucet and made a circle near the drain. He noticed that the circle went one direction —like a clock does. He turned the faucet off and turned it on again. It happened again! Just like a clock! Off and on, again and again—always the same. He forgot about his hands, as the faucet and sink became his lab. Off—on—off—on. He thought he caught the water going the other direction once. He turned it on and off really fast, and the water seemed momentarily confused. But every other time—always the same, always clockwise.

"Jacob?"

"Yes, Mama?"

"Where are you? Dinner's ready? Are those hands clean?"

"Yes, Mama." He hadn't actually put his hands in the water. He turned off the water, and went down the hall, seating himself at the table. "Daddy?"

"Mmm?"

"You should see what I saw. Every time I turned on the water, it always went down the drain in the same way. Always like a clock. I tried it a thousand times. Maybe ten thousand. And every time—the same. Have you seen that, Daddy?"

"Mmmm—hmm."

"Daddy?"

"Dinner, Jacob." His mother put his plate in front of him. "Dad's reading the stock reports." She retreated to her phone. She had to check her work emails. "Never enough time," she sighed. His father remained absorbed in his newspaper.

Jacob ate silently. Water was circling drains and its story needed to be found out.

God's will... Jacob lifted his head staring at the wall.

God's will be done. Why had the wall said this?

After dinner, Jacob returned to his room. It was here he loved to be—the place it was fun to go, where he was a knight and did wonderful things. His toy soldiers and cars lined up as he rode down the promenade, on his horse. Trumpets sounded and banners streamed, for Sir Jacob was returning from adventure! Ladies waved with their cloths, men smiled and saluted. Even children stopped their play to watch as Jacob passed, sitting tall astride his horse.

Jacob smiled and waved back to everyone. He paid attention to even the smallest child, and winked when one of them caught his eye. Flowers fell as if from the sky, sprinkling his saddle in front of him. He would occasionally pick one up and give it to a lady, who blushed, covered her face, and curtsied in response.

He reached the castle—beautiful Dun Aoibhneas!—and dismounted. Ascending the stairs, he shed his armor and weapons, handing them to his squire, Robin. In the Great Hall: more banners and people, and his King, Methred the Tall sitting there, smiling, knowing Jacob's return was a good thing for all involved. Methred and Jacob had grown up together, almost since birth. Was it only that long? It seemed longer than life itself—as if they had been intertwined like a vine and an ancient tree, sentinels of multiple generations. Yet, they were only in their 20's, not long in the tooth, hair, or experience. But they held counsel for each other in a way only the eldest of friends do.

Jacob smiled and sat on the stool near Methred. The court held back their perplexity at the liberties he took with the king for all were happy to have Jacob once again in the castle, and all knew Methred was happiest when Jacob was home. They were kindred spirits, and kindred spirits were not held to the rituals of court. They had grown up together, trained together, learned together, fought together, beaten each other in foot races and horse races, and been at one another's side since the beginning. The beginning of what, really? Perhaps—of time itself. The wizened advisors of the court said it seemed they were two halves of the same soul.

"Jacob?" A female voice called down the hall. It's time to get ready for bed, dear."

Jacob heard the words as if they were ghostly echoes down an ancient hall—words that carried time and deeper meanings. Methred began to fade in front of him, the stool Jacob sat on became his desk chair, and the bright sun of the castle turned into the twilight of evening.

ANTHONY

The family was ready to receive the procession. Mr. and Mrs. Shorter and their two daughters made way for the Bishop and Anthony as they entered the front door. The Bishop made the sign of the cross over the door, hall, and house itself, then sprinkled it all with Holy water. Mr. Shorter and his wife Armena led the Bishop and Anthony down the hall to the basement stair. The stair was surrounded with rich oak wood and trim, the way a central grand stair might be. The house had been built to be the height of luxury, but this was not on the minds of the small party as it proceeded downstairs. Down they went, around the corner, until they came upon the cell. This one was smaller than most—just 12 feet square, with a window and a door.

Anthony stood before the door, looking into the cell that would be his world for the rest of his life. Inside the cell were the meager appurtenances prescribed by the Bishop as he followed the Ancrene Wisse—a straw mat, a small chamber pot, a jug for water, a plate for bread and cheese, and several books. A window, barred, looked into the sunny room they had passed in the hall. Anthony looked at it with a combination of fear and beatific joy. His life could be spent communing with God and praying for the world! He felt closer to God now than at any time in his vocation or training. He was on the verge of a great mission, and he was thankful for this space, this commission, and this – trial – that was to be his life.

He stepped inside as the Bishop began his *aves.*

The door was closed, bolted from the outside. To the sound of the *pater noster,* the heads were sawed off the bolts so that it would require extensive labor over many days to remove the door. There would be no idle leaving on Anthony's part.

Anthony fell to his knees as the Shorters and the Bishop concluded their Glorias. He bowed his head in gratitude. He was home!

THE ANNOUNCEMENT

"Jacob, dear?" His mother still wore the slim black skirt and white blouse she wore most days to work. Her only concession to walking through the door at the end of the day was to remove the black heels she wore every day.

"Yes, Mama?" Jacob lowered his toy horse to the table.

"Your father and I have something to tell you."

Mama never referred to Daddy as "your father." Something was up.

At the table, his father nodded and removed his glasses, laying them on the table by a thick white pillar candle.

"You know your father has been taking many business trips?"

Jacob nodded.

"Well, he's been traveling to Minnesota, where he's doing more and more work. So, we thought, rather than have him travel so much, we might just go live where he's working now. What do you think of that?" His mother smiled broadly.

"You mean, leave this house?" Jacob's heart fluttered in his chest. "But I know this house! It's mine! I've always been here!"

"Jacob, there are really wonderful houses in Minnesota. Daddy has been getting very good work there, and we could live in a castle there compared to this small house."

Min-uh-soh-tah, Jacob thought. They lived in California. Was Min-uh-soh-tah even in this country? "Mama?"

"Yes, dear?"

"Where is Minna-soda?"

"It's pretty far. It takes four hours to get there on a plane."

Jacob had never been on a plane. He had never even imagined being on a plane. He also didn't have a great idea of hours, or time, or whatever it was called. Time seemed to be one of those things that just kind of slipped away on him. He had gotten into trouble often enough for "wasting time," and "running out of time," and other things he didn't really know the meaning of. But, it was clear this "time" concept was really important to adults. That he knew. "Is that like four hours walking?" he asked. "Or four hours in a car?"

His father laughed. "A plane flies *much* faster than a car can drive. Faster than a train."

"Like a dragon? Dragons can catch anything they want to," Jacob said. "What if a dragon catches a plane?"

Jacob's father spoke up. "Son, I can tell you in all my flying, a dragon has never caught one of my planes."

"But it *could* happen."

"Actually, Jacob, I think they designed the planes to be faster than the fastest dragon."

Jacob doubted that. He *knew* about dragons. There was that time he and Methred rode to face the fiercest red dragon of them all, and it wasn't easy! No matter what they did, that red dragon shot fire, flew faster than they could ride, and did everything to tell them it couldn't be defeated. The dragon won that particular fight, but it would not win the war...Jacob and Methred would see to that.

"Jacob?"

Jacob blinked. The red dragon faded away and his mother stared at him. Her eyebrows dipped down over her eyes as if she'd spoken several times. "Yes, Mama?" he said.

"We've found a really nice house in Minnesota. We'll move in June and you can start first grade in St. Paul."

God's Will Be Done.

Back in his room, the words came again. Like a low rumble from the wall, the voice spoke as if from outside, and yet inside. Jacob looked hard at the wall. The wall fell silent.

Jacob lay on his bed. The room was dark, except for the lights outside shining through the window. A breeze rustled the curtains. The smell of so many wonderful flowers came in through the window. The sprinklers around the neighborhood started to turn on, filling his room with the sound of misting water and sprinkler heads starting. Jacob heard the droplets bounce off the leaves of a broad-leafed plant, or the trunk of a palm tree, as the sprinkler went one way and then another. It was a peaceful sound that turned his thoughts to Dun Aoibhneas.

"Jacob! How goes the struggle, my good and finest knight?"

"Methred! Indeed, it goes well. I am unscathed from our latest battle with the Red Dragon. We think we shall soon be able to advance upon him."

"Excellent! This menace must be brought to heel, Sir Jacob! Let no one in this court think otherwise! The very kingdom itself is threatened by this infernal creature!"

Those in the court this fine afternoon bowed, all eyes trained on Jacob, as he reported from the field. As with all courts, there were those who follow the king faithfully, and those with other plans.

But there was no intrigue tonight. Jacob was not only an accomplished knight, but a popular one. Whatever anyone might think of the king, all wished Jacob well. The king, the kingdom, and the people themselves, all benefited from Jacob's courage and skill.

THE NEW HOUSE

Jacob climbed from his father's Mercedes to stare up at the big stone house on the hill. It was enormous—and so red! He thought of the Red Dragon. A huge church—mama called it a *cathedral*—was just down the street. Mama spoke of it as if it was important—as if *they* were important for living so close to it. Jacob didn't understand why. His mother often scoffed at church and God. "That's for weak people too afraid to live life on their own," she would say. So shouldn't she be unhappy to have a big church so close?

"Jacob?" His father's voice cut through his thoughts as if he'd spoken more than once.

Jacob looked up. "Yes, Dad?"

"Your mother asked what you think of the house."

It was *big*, Jacob thought, with a wide front and a huge turret that rose two stories and a window looking down from way up on the third floor and there was a basement, too. Mama had called it a *cellar* and laughed. It wasn't so big as Dun Aoibhneas—but then a hundred people lived in Dun Aoibhneas. "It's very big for three of us," he said. He wished, as he sometimes did, that he had brothers and sisters.

His mother sniffed in the way she sometimes did, a quick sniff that meant she wasn't entirely happy with what someone said. "Summit Hill is the place to be. You'll meet the best people here —people who have money and make things happen. That opens doors to you in the future when you become a lawyer like your father." She put a hand on his head. "You'll love it!"

"Will I get lost inside?" Jacob asked.

His mother laughed. "Not for long."

It didn't reassure him. He remembered the first time he'd wandered the halls of Methred's castle. He'd been quite young, of course. He'd gotten lost in the twisting halls and a servant girl had had to lead him back to the great hall.

"Let's go, Champ," his father said. "You're gonna love this. You love the stories of castles, after all, and this even has ruins in the back!"

"Ruins?" Jacob asked.

His father grabbed his hand, pulling him swiftly down the short sidewalk and up the red stone stairs. At their side, his mother pulled a key from her purse and opened the front door.

"What are ruins?" Jacob asked.

"When a castle or a cathedral has fallen down," his father answered. "When just some of the stone walls are left."

His mother pushed open the door. At the same time, an image flashed before Jacob's eyes of Dun Aoibhneas—the roof gone, the floors gone—only stark stone walls reaching for the sky with empty eyes where glass had once filled the windows. His heart pounded faster.

"Why would a castle fall down?" he demanded. An image filled his mind of the Red Dragon scorching his beautiful castle. "What happened to the people inside?"

"Richard, why do you bring these things up?" his mother

demanded. "You know how he is. Jacob, come in and see your new house! Nothing's happened to anyone." She flung the door wide and Jacob felt dizzy for a second, staring at the vast hall inside. There was a fireplace almost as big as those in Methred's great hall. A marble floor! A ceiling with designs on it. A massive staircase and heavy wooden paneled doors that slid right into the walls!

"Want me to show you around?" His father beamed.

Jacob nodded eagerly. His father was usually too busy for such things—for anything.

"Richard, we have a lot of work to do," his mother said.

"Yes, Faith." His dad sighed, looking at the walls of boxes piled high. "Okay, Champ. Go look around. Pick what bedroom you want. There's one in the basement—I'm guessing you don't want that—and a few on the second floor and a couple in the attic. There's a ballroom up there."

"For basket ball or baseball?" Jacob asked.

"They held dances there." His mother was already working at the tape holding a box together, her back to him.

Jacob waited, hoping his father would change his mind. The place was huge.

"Richard." His mother's voice came out sharply. "These boxes aren't going to unpack themselves. I have to meet my new supervisor tomorrow and I don't want to live like this for the next six months."

Jacob turned to wander through the house.

The house *was* big—but it wasn't so hard to find his way around as Jacob had feared. It helped, of course, that he'd learned to navigate Dun Aoibhneas, quickly understanding it was really just a big square. This house wasn't so different. The kitchen was a huge room with stone walls off the living room where his parents worked at the boxes. Upstairs, all the bedrooms easily flowed back into the hallway where a large dark banister looked down into the rooms below and lined broad stairs.

He wandered in and out of the bedrooms. One of them had a big fireplace—though not so big as the ones in his castle. His parents' bed stood in front of the big bay windows of the second floor of the tower room. Boxes were piled high against the walls.

He crossed back over the hall to another bedroom—more bow windows, his own bed. Another hall led to a big sun room. He pressed his nose to the screen, looking down into the yard of the house next door. A girl stood on the roof of the porch. She glanced at him, waved, and leapt off. Jacob gasped.

She landed on a trampoline below and bounced—one, two, three times, laughing in glee.

Then Jacob noticed four boys running around the yard. One of them scrambled up onto the trampoline and began bouncing, too, grinning and waving at Jacob every time he flew up in the air.

Jacob ducked away. He didn't know how to make new friends. He'd always had his friends in his neighborhood and school. Always! He ran from the room, down the big, wide staircase, and all the way down to the basement—the cellar as his mother called it. She laughed every time she said it.

There he stopped in surprise. He didn't know what he expected, but it wasn't this! Cellars, he thought, were dark and dreary like the dungeons of Dun Aoibhneas.

But this! This looked like the country club his father took them to in California. Sconces pooled soft light on dark elegant paneling on the walls. A deep crimson runner unfurled the length the hall floor. Jacob dropped to his knees, touching the stone floor that showed on either side of the carpet. He climbed to his feet, looking around. There was a large room at the end of the hall. He proceeded slowly down the long hall, looking up in wonder at the paneling worthy even of Methred's castle, to the crown molding at the top. Several doors lined the hall. He dared not look in them, lest he find dragons guarding treasure.

At the end, the hall opened into a large room, its walls of

white-washed cement. White iron racks ran around the walls, full of lush, green plants. A bed stood in the center. Mama had said the previous owners had left some things. Jacob studied the room closely. It had wide, narrow windows at the tops of the walls that spilled in tons of sunshine. One of them was open and he could hear the children next door laughing.

He crept closer to the bed. It had an old-fashioned white iron frame and a heavy quilt that seemed to have come from a long-ago era.

Thy will be done.

Jacob spun! Eyes wide, he scanned the room. It was empty.

Behind the greenery, he suddenly realized a stair disappeared into the wall. It looked like the stairs in Dun Aoibhneas—the one behind the throne that almost no one knew about. Jacob inched up to it, peering in and up. He could hear his mother's voice somewhere above, directing his father to put the china away while she attended a work meeting online—it was vitally important—and be sure to sort sorting out *those tools of his* in the garage. "We don't have much room out there," she said. "It'll have to be well-organized to leave space for the car."

Jacob trod quietly up the stairs. They turned inside the wall, arriving at a narrow opening into the grand living room just to the right of the front door.

Unwrapping the good china, his father said, "I thought I'd take Jacob out to see the ruins after this box."

"We have plenty of time for that later." His mother called back over her shoulder as she headed to the room that would be her office, "These things need to be done."

Jacob stood quietly by the wall.

"True." His father stared after his mother, shook his head sadly, and returned to his work.

Jacob backed down the stairs, back into the sunny basement room. He walked around, studying the plants that thrived inexplicably, and running a hand over the old quilt. It had four large panels. The upper right showed two black horses facing each other from either side of a tree. The lower left showed one proud black stallion. The upper left had a white dog in the center of a laurel wreath while its opposite square showed a white horse and a white dog looking at each other in front of a big white two-story house beside a tree.

His mother wouldn't like it. She would certainly replace it with something bright and new. That made Jacob sad. He wondered who had made it. He touched the big white farmhouse —he knew it was a farmhouse, somehow—what else could it be? Was it the house of whoever made the quilt? Was that their dog in the bed cover?

Had those horses existed? He stared into the tiny black knots of thread that were their eyes.

Pepper. Lee.

Jacob smiled. "Hi, Pepper. Hi, Lee. You should come to Dun Aoibhneas with me. Methred could use a fine pair of horses like you." He thought maybe he'd take the quilt—hide it in his room before Mama saw it and threw it out.

Barkee! Jacob's smile grew, as his eyes turned to the white dog. He almost imagined it wagged its tail. "You, too," he said. "Did your boy get old?" It had to have been a boy, probably his own age, who named the dog Barkee.

Thy will be done.

Jacob spun again. With the horses and the dog reassuring him —he felt they were telling him, *It's okay, he's our friend!* – Jacob ran into the hall. On his right, a broad pair of doors with dozens of small glass panes opened into a bright, sunny room, its windows, too, were higher up on the walls, but bigger than in the other room. A door led to the outside. Going to the door, Jacob could see stairs leading up to the lawn, and a large stone fountain much like that in Methred's courtyard, and gardens full of colorful flowers.

He turned back to the interior. The room held what seemed to be hundreds of green plants—almost a jungle! They sat on low tables by the window, on a tall granite-topped table in the middle of the room, on shelves on the walls!

Jacob laughed out loud at the life in the room. He flung his arms out, spinning in a circle and dancing around the big table, with plants and lush greenery on either side and sunlight pouring in the window. How could a basement room have windows to the outside?

"They are beautiful, aren't they?"

Jacob stopped as quickly as he'd started.

"He said you'd be coming."

Jacob turned slowly. This side of the room had the same dark wood paneling as the hall. Only now—he saw the window in the paneling. A small *hiss* sounded, and a panel slid, exposing the full size of a large window with bars across it.

Jacob took a step closer.

A man sat inside, smiling out at him. "You *are* Jacob, aren't you?" he asked.

Jacob gasped. Then he quickly said, "It's you Pepper and Lee and Barkee meant. They said not to be scared of you."

The man beamed. "Good horses. A fine dog."

Jacob could see, as his eyes adjusted to the dim light inside the cell, that the man was bald on the top of his head. He seemed a little older than his father, but not much. And he wore a heavy brow robe with a cowl around his shoulders. "Are you a Cistercian?" Jacob asked. The Cistercians worked and prayed at Dun Aoibhneas..

"I am indeed! My name is Anthony. I'm pleased to meet you."

Jacob cocked his head. "Why are you in our walls?"

"Mr. and Mrs. Shorter wanted an anchorite to pray for their family."

"Who are they?"

"They lived here long ago."

"Like a hundred years ago?"

Anthony tilted his head, frowning. "Not quite so long as that. They lived to be quite old—well into the 1930s."

"But why are you still here?"

"It is what I do. I live in my hermitage and pray for the families in this house as I strive to become a saint."

"What is a saint?"

"One who is very holy and close to God."

Before Jacob could say more, he heard his mother's voice coming from the stairs. "Jacob! Jacob, where are you? It's time to go visit your new school!"

"I'll be back!" Jacob mounted his ebony horse, Pepper, and with Barkee racing at his side, galloped up the stairs, almost crashing into his mother. "Mama!" he cried, "there's a man in our walls down there!"

"What took you so long?" she asked.

"Mama, there's a…."

"I heard you," she said. "Stop this nonsense. You know there are no men in the walls just like there's no Methred." She squatted down, perched carefully on her heels in her slim black skirt. The red garnet pin flashed on her lapel. She took his hands in hers. "Jacob, you really are getting too old to have imaginary friends. You're going into first grade."

"But Mama, it's true. He said he's trying to be a saint. We have a saint in our cellar!"

Mama rose in one fluid motion to her elegant height above him. "Jacob, there is absolutely no one there," she said as she turned to reach for the car keys.

"He said Mr. and Mrs. Shorter asked him in. They died in the 1930s when they were in their 80s."

She stopped. She turned slowly, looking down at him. "How do you know about the Shorters?"

Jacob's lower lip trembled just for a second as he stared at his mother in surprise. She didn't believe him! "I just told you. Anthony told me about them."

Mama spun and marched, her heels click-clacking on the parquet wooden floor. "Richard?" Raising her voice she called into the living room. "Richard, did you tell Jacob about the Shorters?"

Daddy stuck his head out around a pile of boxes that reached up to the ceiling. "No, Faith." He looked surprised. "Why in the world would I be talking about the Shorters?"

Mama drew in her little sniff, and click-clacked back to Jacob, taking his hand and leading him out the front door onto the broad red stone porch. "You need to stop the fanciful stories."

Thy will be done.

Jacob heard the words and he felt he saw Anthony smiling. He felt Pepper prancing along beside him. He would make a fine steed at Dun Aoibhneas. He beamed up at his mother. "Yes, Mama!"

He couldn't wait to run down to the basement and talk to Anthony again.

Resources

I hope you've enjoyed the stories! Below are a few resources related to things talked about in the stories herein.

Anchorites/Anchoresses:

Ancrene Wisse - Articles - Hermitary

https://formrage.com/ebook/ancrene-wisse

French Lore:

https://www.talkinfrench.com/15-supernatural-french-creatures-you-havent-heard-of-a-pre-halloween-special/

King Herla:

https://bluebellstrilogy.blogspot.com/2016/09/the-mysterious-story-of-king-herla.html

Time Slips:

https://anomalien.com/the-mystery-of-time-slips-real-cases-and-theories/

Trail of Tears:

https://www.nps.gov/trte/learn/historyculture/laughlin-park-exhibits.htm

William of Newburgh:

https://discover.hubpages.com/education/The-Vampires-and-Zombies-of-William-of-Newburgh

You can find more tales of the mysterious, time travel, legend, lore, Scotland, and medieval times at my blog:

https://bluebellstrilogy.blogspot.com

Connect with me at www.lauravosika.com or at facebook:

www.facebook.com/laura.vosika.author

Find me also at:

www.booksandbrews.net

Wordsmiths and a Wolfhound on YouTube

More from Gabriel's Horn

The Feet Say Run Hans Jaeger, trapped on a desert island, recalls his life from 1930s Germany to the present and his possible redemption. By Dan Blum

My Gypsy War Diary An introverted boy stumbles onto a long-buried mystery of love and betrayal—and treasure, stolen and stolen again! By Shawn Brink

Hell on Earth An end-times apocalyptic adventure, the final of the *Space Between* trilogy. By Shawn Brink.

Gypsy Heart The collected poetry of a Hungarian immigrant; a fascinating look into another world. By Lilly Gelle

Shattered Faith When Faith begins having strange visions, she must face that her perfect marriage...is not so perfect. By Rebecca May Hope

Silken Strands One man's utopia is a young girl's

nightmare. A coming of age story of the historic Oneida community. By Rebecca May Hope

A Dream of Dragons Henry finds a helpless young girl on the beach. It is amazing how quickly she learns. But her dreams of golden dragons that turn dark...they *are* only dreams, aren't they? By Lauretta and Michael Kehoe

The Path That Shines Bonnie suffered from multiple health issues—any of which might kill her at any moment. A medical memoir of navigating illness, hospitals, and the loss of a spouse. By Chris R. Powell

On Wings of Love and Light Love lost and love found—a journey in poetry and essays about what love is. By Laura Vosika and Chris R. Powell

Gabriel's Horn Poetry Anthology: new poetry in traditional forms

> *Startled by JOY 2019*
>
> *Startled by NATURE 2020*
>
> *Startled by LOVE 2021*

...and much more from mysteries to memoir to adventure to inspirational, contemporary fiction, paranormal, non-fiction, horror, and more

www.gabrielshornpress.com

Made in the USA
Columbia, SC
04 October 2024

43662390R00093